Sunshine In Her Eyes

Laura Gramer

LITTLE CREEK PRESS
MINERAL POINT, WISCONSIN

Little Creek Press
5341 Sunny Ridge Road
Mineral Point, WI 53565

Printed in the United States of America

Cataloging-in-Publication Data
Name: Laura Gramer, author
Title: Sunshine In Her Eyes
Description: Mineral Point, WI Little Creek Press, 2025
Identifiers: LCCN: 2025919486 | ISBN: 978-1-967311-85-9
Classification: FICTION / Family Life / General
FICTION / Small Town & Rural
FICTION / Literary

Book design by Little Creek Press

This book is dedicated to my dear sister, Olivia Grimm, and Garret Baerwolf.

Olivia, our adventures on our grandparents' farm were the inspiration and foundation of this story. Thank you for being the sweetest childhood playmate a sister could ever hope for. You really are the most thoughtful and talented person I've ever known. I'm grateful to call you my sister and my friend.

Garret, your humor has fueled my creativity during some very monotonous moments of wading through the depths of these pages. Your excitement for and knowledge of farming are both humbling and refreshing.

Together, you both inspired the joy and wonder that shaped this book. Thank you for making this piece possible!

Contents

Bright Horizons

The hum of a summer breeze drifted through the open kitchen window, mingling with the faint aroma of soap and water. Maddie McDowe stood at the sink, her hands submerged in warm, sudsy water, scrubbing the last of the breakfast dishes. The remnants of potato pancakes clung stubbornly to the ceramic plate, while a few stray bits of peppered bacon floated lazily before disappearing down the drain.

She didn't mind washing dishes. In fact, she enjoyed the quiet moment. It gave her a chance to let her thoughts wander freely, like clouds drifting across the vast Wisconsin sky. Through the window, she could see the olive-green pastures stretching out before her, the tall grasses rippling in waves as a warm breeze swept through. The cows lingering across the field, chewed their cud gracefully, swishing their tails to ward off flies.

Her fingers worked, scrubbing and rinsing, but her mind was elsewhere. She was already envisioning her next painting of her beloved cow, Gem-Sparkles, standing in the middle of a lush soybean field, her head crowned with a homemade garland of wildflowers. The idea filled Maddie with excitement, and she mentally mapped out the colors she would use: deep greens and purples for the pasture, a sky brushed with soft blues and golden sunshine, and delicate purples and pinks for the wildflowers.

The McDowe farm had been Maddie's world for sixteen years. Nestled on the outskirts of Marinette, Wisconsin, it was more than just a place to live; it was a piece of her soul. Every inch of the land held a memory. The freestall barn where she had spent countless hours feeding calves with her mom. The old oak tree by the chicken coop where she sat with her favorite hen, Charcoal, stroking her silky feathers. The creek that cut through the pasture where she and her brothers had gone for many swims.

Maddie dried her hands on a dish towel and glanced at the clock. Ten in the morning. Her brothers, Jarred and Paul, were already out in the fields, working the land like they had every summer since they were old enough to drive a tractor. The thought of them made her smile as bright as the sun beaming outside.

Jarred, the eldest, was methodical and hardworking, always thinking five steps ahead. Paul, just a year younger, was the wild spirit: adventurous, strong, and always up for a challenge. Together, they balanced each other out, and Maddie loved them fiercely.

A sudden wave of nostalgia washed over her, making her chest tighten. Time was slipping through her fingers like sand, and she wasn't ready to say goodbye to this season of life. Jarred had been studying for a medical test that would determine whether or not he was ready for medical school. Paul, although still undecided about his future, talked about possibly running the farm full-time.

And then there was Maddie, standing at the kitchen sink, feeling like she was caught between childhood and whatever came next.

Can't You slow time down, Lord? she thought. *Just for a little while? How I do wish for a few more years of us all living on the farm. Couldn't You do that for me ... for us? We'll have the rest of the time You give us here on earth to be adults and live in our own houses.*

She let out a small sigh, shaking away the heaviness settling in her heart. There was still time to enjoy the farm, to be with her brothers, to hold onto this season just a little bit longer.

With renewed determination, Maddie tossed the dish towel over her shoulder and made her way to the pantry. If she couldn't slow time down, she could at least make the most of it. She grabbed and toasted four slices of bread, burning the edges of two because Paul preferred his toast that way. Maddie turned up her nose at the sight of charred carbs. She spread homemade butter made from their cows' milk on the slices of toast, added sliced tomatoes and salami, and packed the sandwiches into Ziploc bags.

A snack run to the fields was definitely in order.

Rhythm of the Land

The late morning sun was climbing higher, stretching golden fingers across the landscape as Maddie stepped outside, the small bundle of sandwiches tucked under her arm. The scent of fresh earth and wildflowers mingled with the more familiar aroma of cow manure, a smell she had long since grown used to. To her, it wasn't unpleasant. It was home.

She made her way to the ATV shed, slipping into her well-worn sloggers before climbing into the Gator. The engine rumbled to life beneath her, and she pulled out of the yard, heading toward the fields where her brothers were working.

The farm was alive with summer's warmth. Birds flitted through the treetops, their songs weaving together with the distant hum of machinery. A few whitetail deer darted through the trees as Maddie drove past, their brown coats blending seamlessly with the dappled sunlight.

She turned onto the dirt path leading to the field where Jarred and Paul were planting soybeans. The tires kicked up small clouds of dust as she neared the tractors, their engines rumbling steadily as they worked the land.

Spotting her, Paul powered down his tractor and leaned against the frame, wiping sweat from his brow. His blond curls were damp, his tanned skin streaked with dust. "If it isn't our favorite delivery service," Paul chuckled, watching his sister, who had a smile as wide as the Cheshire Cat plastered across her face.

Jarred, a little ways off, hopped down from his tractor and stretched his arms above his head. "Tell me you brought something good, Mads."

Maddie grinned, holding up the bag. "Salami and tomato sandwiches. And before you ask, Paul, no, I didn't pack beef sticks. You ate the last one yesterday."

Paul let out an exaggerated sigh. "Tragic."

The three of them settled into a small patch of shade beneath an old oak tree at the edge of the field. The leaves rustled softly above them, offering a brief reprieve from the midday sun.

Maddie passed out the sandwiches, watching as her brothers tore into them with the kind of hunger only farm work could bring.

"You guys are making good progress," she said, glancing out at the freshly planted rows.

Jarred nodded and talked while between bites. "Yeah, another two days and this field should be done."

"Just in time, too. Rain's supposed to hit in four days." Maddie smiled. "I checked the forecast this morning. I figured you'd want to know."

Paul let out a small laugh. "What would we do without you, sis?"

Maddie leaned back against the tree, closing her eyes for a moment as a breeze swept through the fields. She wanted to freeze this moment, to etch it into her memory like one of her paintings. The scent of fresh soil. The sound of wind rustling through the soybeans. The warmth of the sun on her skin.

She opened her eyes, watching as her brothers sat in comfortable silence, their faces tanned from long hours in the field, their hands calloused from years of hard work.

"This," she said softly, almost to herself, "is what I want to remember."

Paul glanced at her, a knowing look in his eyes. "You thinking about painting it?"

A smile tugged at Maddie's lips. "Maybe. I can already see it in my head, how the light hits the fields in the morning, the way the tractors blend into the landscape like they belong there."

Jarred wiped his hands on his jeans, nodding. "You've got an eye for that kind of thing. Can't wait to see what you come up with."

Maddie's cheeks warmed at the compliment. "Thanks."

For a while, they just sat there, soaking in the quiet rhythm of the land. These simple, unspoken moments were what Maddie cherished most, filled with the kind of peace that only the farm could offer.

Eventually, Paul stretched and stood, dusting off his jeans. “Alright, break’s over. Time to get back at it.”

Jarred groaned but followed suit. Maddie stood, too, brushing the crumbs from her lap. “I’ll leave you guys to it,” she said, hopping back into the Gator.

As she drove away, she glanced in the rearview mirror, watching as her brothers climbed back into their tractors, their figures silhouetted against the backdrop of the endless fields.

She had her inspiration. Now, it was time to bring it to life.

A Painter's Perspective

The house was quiet when Maddie returned, the kind of stillness that settled in between the busyness of farm life. Her parents were out running errands, and with her brothers back in the fields, she had the space to herself.

She set the bag of leftover sandwich wrappers on the counter and made her way to the living room, where her easel stood by the wide front window. Morning light still streamed through, casting a soft glow over her painting supplies.

Maddie picked up a paintbrush and turned to her canvas, studying the unfinished scene she had started the week before. The rolling pastures, the sunlit soybean field, and the distant silhouette of the barn were all there, but something was missing.

The moment.

She wanted to capture more than just the scenery. She wanted to paint the feeling of standing in the fields with her brothers, of hearing their laughter, of sensing the weight of the land they loved beneath their feet.

Setting down the brush, she pulled out a fresh canvas. This piece would be different.

Maddie mixed her paints, blending the deep greens of the pasture with the rich browns of the soil. She dabbed her brush in a soft gold, adding warmth to the sky, then swiped a careful stroke of blue for the distant tree line.

She lost herself in the rhythm of painting, each brushstroke drawing her deeper into the memory of the morning. She painted the towering tractors, their sturdy frames standing as a testament to the hard work they put into the land. She added the shadows stretching across the field, the play of light filtering through the leaves of the oak tree where they had sat.

And then, almost without thinking, she began painting Paul leaning against his tractor, grinning as he wiped his hands on his jeans, and Jarred standing beside him, quiet and steady, always thinking, always planning.

It wasn't perfect yet, but it was real and raw and right from the heart.

Maddie stepped back, wiping a stray streak of green paint from her cheek.

Her stomach growled, reminding her that she hadn't eaten since breakfast. With a sigh, she set the brush down and wandered into the kitchen. A quick peanut butter and honey sandwich would do.

As she ate, she let her mind drift.

She had always loved painting, but lately, it felt like more than just a hobby. It was a way to hold onto the things that mattered, to preserve them before time carried them away.

Maybe that was why she wasn't ready to grow up.

The thought made her chest ache. She knew change was coming, whether she liked it or not. Jarred was preparing for medical school. Paul had been taking on more responsibility on the farm. Maddie would perfect her gift in painting and one day maybe even get married to an adventurous boy who loves God. Whatever the future held, one thing was certain: They would all move out, journeying on their own paths.

Maddie pushed the thought aside. She didn't want to think about it yet.

She rinsed her plate and returned to the living room, where her painting waited. The scene was coming together, but it still lacked something.

Then, she knew.

She dipped her brush into a soft lavender hue and carefully added the final touch: a crown of wildflowers for Gem-Sparkles, who stood in the corner of the field, as if watching over everything.

Another small smile tugged at her lips. Yes. That was it.

Kindred Spirits

It was the first day back to school from summer vacation. The school hallway smelled like a mixture of warm cheese sandwiches and poster paint. Maddie walked through it, her backpack slung over one shoulder, her sketchbook tucked under her arm. The chatter of students laughing, teasing, and complaining about assignments filled the space. She usually didn't mind the noise, but today it felt overwhelming.

She had spent the entire bus ride picturing her nearly finished painting, wondering if she should add more detail to the sky or adjust the shading in the soybean field. It had been hard to focus on anything else.

But now, as she approached her locker, she felt the shift in atmosphere before she even saw them—Macy and JoAnna Pewasta.

The sisters leaned casually against the lockers a few feet away, their arms crossed, eyes scanning the hallway like they owned it. Maddie had learned to ignore them, but that never stopped them from trying to get under her skin.

"Oh, look. The little farm girl's back from the fields," Macy said, her voice just loud enough for Maddie to hear. "Smell anything, JoAnna?"

JoAnna wrinkled her nose. "Hard to tell if it's cow manure or just her."

Maddie took a slow breath, focusing on the lock in front of her. *Don't react.* That was the rule she had made for herself years ago. If she didn't react, they would get bored. She turned the combination, opening her locker with careful movements.

But Macy wasn't finished. "Did you bring your little doodles with you again?" she asked, tilting her head toward the sketchbook in Maddie's arms. "You know, I bet the cows just love your artwork. Maybe they even eat it."

JoAnna let out a laugh, flipping her sleek ponytail over her shoulder. "Jarred's the only good thing that came from that family. The rest are just ... rural."

Maddie clenched her jaw. That one stung, not for herself but for Paul. She hated when they spoke like he wasn't worth noticing, like his hard work on the farm meant nothing.

Before she could stop herself, she turned her head slightly, meeting JoAnna's gaze. "You sound a little obsessed with my brother."

It wasn't much, but it was enough. JoAnna's eyes narrowed, and her posture stiffened, like a cat bristling before a fight. Maddie didn't stick around to see what she would say next. She grabbed her books, slammed her locker shut, and walked away.

She didn't care what they thought of her. Not really. But that didn't mean it didn't hurt.

By the time lunch rolled around, the tension had faded. Maddie found her usual seat at the table by the windows, where Liza was already waiting.

"There you are!" Liza said, her blue eyes bright. She reached into her lunch bag and pulled out a plastic container of chocolate chip cookies. "I may or may not have snuck extras from the batch my mom made last night."

Maddie smiled, accepting one. "You are my favorite person today."

Liza grinned. "Aren't I your favorite person every day?"

"Yes, Liza!"

The best friends looked at each other sweetly, trying to contain themselves in public, but it was no use, as their wells of silliness bubbled up in the form of uncontrollable laughter.

Everyone else in the cafeteria gazed at the girls because of their spontaneous outbursts.

When their pulses slowed, they resumed eating in comfortable silence for a moment, watching the leaves outside sway in the breeze. Then, Liza nudged Maddie's arm. "Okay. You're doing that thing where you think too hard. What's up?"

Maddie hesitated, then sighed. "Macy and JoAnna." Liza rolled her eyes. "What did they say this time?"

Maddie recalled their words. She kept her voice light, not wanting to give the Pewasta sisters more power than they deserved.

Liza's face darkened. "Oh, those two must just wake up in the morning and choose cruelty."

Maddie shrugged. "I don't care what they think about me."

Liza gave her a knowing look. "But you do care when they talk about Paul."

Maddie sighed. "Yeah."

Liza leaned forward, her expression serious. "Listen, you and I both know Paul is one of the best people on this planet. And so do our families. Macy and JoAnna? They don't matter."

Maddie knew Liza was right, but her words still lingered.

To lighten the mood, Liza changed the subject. "So, any updates on the masterpiece?"

Maddie perked up. "Almost done. Just a few more details." Liza grinned. "I want to be the first non-McDowe to see it." "You've got a deal."

Liza, with her eyes sparkling, leaned in, clearly eager to share something.

"You won't believe what Max-a-million did last night," she said, trying to hold back a powerful belly laugh.

Maddie raised an eyebrow, intrigued. "What now?"

Liza couldn't suppress a grin. "He tried to climb a tree ..." She paused dramatically, glancing around as if sharing a secret. "But it was the tree that had the better idea. He ended up stuck, hanging upside down like a squirrel, and my dad had to rescue him."

Maddie giggled, nearly spilling her carton of milk. "That cat of yours is too silly!"

Liza chuckled, nodding her head. “So, what’s your plan for this weekend? Unless you’re going to paint all weekend, we could do something spontaneous.”

“Oooo. Absolutely!”

“I was thinking we could go out on the four-wheelers. We could go racing with everyone!”

Maddie’s face lit up. “I’m in. Maybe we could head out to the old trails by the creek. It’s been a while since I’ve had a real adventure.”

Liza nodded, her eyes glimmering with excitement. “That sounds perfect. It’s about time we did something out of the ordinary, don’t you think?”

Maddie smirked. “You know me. I’m all about the unexpected.” By the time the bell rang, Maddie felt a little lighter.

The Pewasta sisters weren’t worth her time.

Muck Monsters

The weekend came and Maddie sat on the front porch tying the laces of her old sneakers, the ones already stained with dirt from years of summer adventures. The warm breeze carried the scent of cut hay and damp earth, mingling with the distant sound of a tractor somewhere across the farm.

She could already hear the distant hum of four-wheelers approaching, a telltale sign that the Lerians had arrived. Maddie jumped to her feet just as a cloud of dust rose from the driveway.

Greyson, Allison, and Liza piled off the four-wheeler, their faces lit with excitement. Behind them, James pulled up on another, giving Maddie a lazy salute.

"Ready to get dirty, McDowe?" he called. Maddie grinned. "Always."

Paul walked out of the barn, tossing his work gloves onto a bale of hay. "Took you long enough."

Liza rolled her eyes. “Some of us had to wait for a certain someone to fix a broken chain on the four-wheeler before we could leave.”

Greyson held up his hands in defense. “Not my fault! Okay ... maybe it was. But at least I fixed it.”

Paul chuckled. “Good. Wouldn’t want you making excuses when I leave you in the dust.”

Greyson scoffed. “Oh, it’s on, Paul-ey boy.”

Maddie laughed as they all walked toward the shed where the rest of the four-wheelers were parked. Jarred had stayed behind, too busy with his studies to join them, but Maddie knew he would have loved a day like this.

They split into teams of two, including Maddie and James, Paul and Liza, Greyson and Allison, and each climbed onto their rides. The helmets, a gift from Maddie’s parents, were passed around, and she smiled at the familiar weight of hers as she strapped it on.

“All right,” James said, revving the engine. “Race to the east side of the woods, then to the mud hole. First team there gets bragging rights.”

Maddie grinned, gripping the sides of the four-wheeler as James took off, the wind whipping through her hair. The dirt path blurred beneath them, the familiar rush of speed sending a thrill through her chest.

Behind them, she could hear Paul and Liza gaining.

James glanced over his shoulder. “They’re catching up, McDowe.”

“Take the shortcut through the trees!” Maddie shouted. James grinned, steering the four-wheeler off the main trail, weaving through the thick underbrush. Branches whipped past them, but Maddie leaned into the turns, trusting James' driving.

When they burst out of the trees onto the main trail again, Paul and Liza were just ahead.

Maddie laughed. "Told you it would work!"

They reached the clearing near the mud hole at almost the same time. Greyson and Allison, however, were nowhere to be seen.

Paul parked his four-wheeler, shaking his head. "Where'd those two go?"

Just then, a loud splat filled the air, followed by laughter.

Greyson and Allison came flying toward them, already covered in mud. Their four-wheeler hit a deep patch, spraying mud everywhere, and Maddie barely had time to shield herself before she felt the cold, wet splatter across her arms.

Liza groaned, wiping mud from her cheek. "Greyson!"

Greyson grinned. "Hey, you don't come mudding to stay clean." Paul laughed. "Guess that means we're getting in, too."

And with that, the games began.

The engines roared to life, and one after another they tore through the thick, sticky mud. Tires gritted into the ground, sending plumes of water and dirt into the air like a storm had hit. The four-wheelers lurched, sliding sideways before gripping the earth again, their engines whining under the strain. Laughter echoed above the chaos, but soon, it was drowned out by the sound of splashing, mud soaking into clothes, plastering faces, and clinging to every inch of exposed skin. The once-dusty trail was now a river of brown, and everyone, covered in muck, looked like they'd been through a downpour of dirt.

They all heaved for air. Maddie wiped a hand across her face, smearing mud into her hair. James hopped off the ATV and held out his hand, offering it to Maddie. "Always a pleasure riding with you, McDowe." James caught Maddie's gaze.

Liza walked over and sat beside Maddie, who panted from excitement.

"I think we officially look like muck monsters," Maddie said.

James flopped onto the grass beside them. "Best. Day. Ever. To. Be. Alive."

Maddie couldn't help but smile and yawn.

As the sun started to sink lower in the sky, they reluctantly packed up, riding back to the farm in their mud-soaked clothes. Maddie knew her mother would shake her head at the sight of them, muttering about "her little cavemen" needing to wash off before stepping foot inside.

But she wouldn't trade this day for anything. For now, they were still young. Free. And that was enough, at least, for now.

Down in the Creek

By the time Maddie got back to the house, the mud had dried in thick patches on her jeans and arms. Her hair was a tangled mess, streaked with dirt where she had wiped her face earlier.

As expected, her mother took one look at her from the front porch and let out a dramatic sigh. "My little caveman," Dara muttered, shaking her head. "Straight to the creek before you even think about coming inside."

Maddie grinned. "Yes, Ma!"

She jogged toward the creek, hearing the others laughing as they did the same. The cool water rushed past her hands as she knelt at the edge, scrubbing the mud from her arms and splashing her face.

Paul dunked his head under, shaking out his curls when he surfaced. "Ahh. Nothing like a good mud bath followed by a creek rinse."

Liza sat nearby, wringing out the ends of her braid. "That was the best day ever," she said, her voice full of contentment.

Maddie nodded. "Yeah. It really was."

But even as she smiled, that ache of nostalgia crept back in. There wouldn't always be days like this.

Paul would take on more responsibilities with the farm. Jarred would leave for medical school. Liza might move away one day, too.

And then what?

Would these moments just be memories, tucked away like old photographs?

Maddie hated how quickly time was slipping through her fingers.

When she got back to the house, freshly cleaned and wrapped in one of her father's oversized flannels, she curled up on the couch with her sketchbook. She flipped past old portraits of her brothers, sketches of the barn at sunrise, and studies of Gem-Sparkles' expressive eyes.

Then, on a blank page, she started a new drawing.

She sketched the outline of the four-wheelers first, then added the figures of her friends: Liza laughing, Paul splattered in mud, and Greyson standing triumphantly with his arms raised like a champion.

She worked for over an hour, shading in the details, capturing the motion and life in the scene.

When she was done, she held the sketch at arm's length.

It wasn't just a picture. It was a way of holding onto today. A way of making sure she wouldn't forget.

Maddie ran her fingers over the pencil lines, feeling a deep sense of satisfaction.

A creak of the old farmhouse floor made her look up. Her mother walked into the room, setting her Bible and a notebook down on the dining table. Maddie watched as Dara sank into a chair, rubbing her temples before letting out a small sigh.

"You okay, Mom?" Maddie asked, closing her sketchbook.

Dara gave her a tired smile. "Just running through everything before we leave tomorrow. You know how it is. I always feel like I'm forgetting something."

Maddie sat up straighter. "Wait, you leave tomorrow? Where are you going?"

Dara chuckled. "Yes, Maddie. We told you about this last week. The church seminar in Illinois? Your dad has to represent the elders, and I'm going with him."

Maddie vaguely remembered them mentioning something about a trip, but it hadn't really registered at the time. "How long will you be gone?"

"Four days," her mother replied. "It's an important conference, and your dad felt called to go. A few of the other church elders were planning to attend, but something came up, so he'll be the only one representing."

Maddie processed that for a moment. Four days wasn't a long time, but it was just enough to make things feel ... different.

"You and Paul will be in charge of things while we're gone," Dara continued. "Jarred will still be busy studying, but he'll help where he can. We've got the chores listed out, and Cari said she'd stop by if you need anything."

Maddie nodded. She wasn't worried about managing the farm. She and the boys had done it plenty of times before. But there was something about her parents' leaving that made her chest feel tight. It was probably because she had been thinking so much about time, about change.

"Don't look so concerned," her mother said gently. "You and Paul will do great, like always. And we'll only be a phone call away."

Maddie forced a smile. "I know. I'll just miss you so."

"Oh, dear one." Her mother gracefully stood up from her chair and walked over to her daughter, pulling her into a sweet embrace.

Firelight Shadows

"Bye, my darlings," Dara said, squeezing them one last time. "Paul, per your request, we didn't ask anyone to come help with chores, but remember, the Lerians are just down the road if you need anything."

Paul nodded. "We've got it covered, Mom. You and Dad just enjoy yourselves."

Maddie stepped back, smiling. "Yeah, Mom. You deserve a break. Don't think about the farm. Just focus on having fun with Dad."

Jarred clapped his dad on the back. "Loosen up, old man. Enjoy yourself."

Tyler chuckled, his laugh lines deepening. "I'll do my best. Just don't burn the house down while we're gone."

With that, Dara and Tyler climbed into the salamander-colored truck, and Maddie, Paul, and Jarred stood on the porch, waving as their parents disappeared down the road.

The moment the truck was out of sight, Jarred turned

to his siblings with a grin. "So, what do you guys wanna do first? Donkey basketball game downtown? Eat Chinese food?"

Paul smirked. "I thought you had to study," he said and motioned to Jarred.

"Let's make homemade pizza and play Twister!" Maddie cut in excitedly.

"Competitive Twister and pizza? This is gonna get messy."

The kitchen buzzed with activity as they got to work. Maddie rolled out the dough, her hands dusted with flour. Jarred, chopping vegetables, glanced up. "Hey, Mads, you want your mushrooms sliced or diced?"

Maddie scrunched her nose. "Jarred, yuck."

"Ahh, just gotta mess with you," he teased, grinning.

Paul, stirring a pot of rich homemade pizza sauce, gave an approving nod. "Mom sure does grow the best tomatoes. The sauce is ready!"

The three of them worked seamlessly. Jarred stretched the dough, Paul spread the sauce, and Maddie layered on the cheese and toppings. By the time the pizzas were in the oven, they were already setting up the Twister mat.

Laughter filled the living room as they twisted and contorted, each move making balance more difficult. "Right hand, yellow!" Paul called, barely containing his giggles as Maddie wobbled dangerously.

"You so rigged that spin!" she protested, her arms shaking as she tried to hold her position.

Despite Maddie's attempts to throw Jarred off, he remained focused. His dark hair hung over his eyes as he gritted his teeth in determination.

Then Maddie, unable to hold back her laughter, collapsed onto the mat in a heap. That was all it took. Jarred lost his balance, toppling onto her, followed by Paul. The three of them lay tangled together, breathless from laughter.

When the oven timer beeped, Paul scrambled up and pulled out the pizzas, the golden cheese bubbling perfectly. Their first bites were met with delighted hums of approval. It was a perfect evening, with good food, good company, and the comforting normalcy of home.

As they finished eating, Maddie stretched her arms over her head. "I think I'm going to sleep in the barn tonight."

Paul raised an eyebrow. "You serious?"

She nodded. "It's on my bucket list. I think tonight's the perfect night."

Jarred shrugged. "You want Paul and me to join you?"

Maddie smiled. "Nah, I'll be fine. But thanks."

She grabbed a thin blanket and made her way to the freestall barn, the warm summer air thick with the scent of hay and cows. Nestling beside her pet cow, Gem-Sparkles, Maddie lay down, feeling the steady rise and fall of the animal's breathing.

The barn was peaceful. Moonlight filtered through the wooden slats, casting a deep silver shadow across the hay-strewn floor. Maddie let out a soft sigh, feeling a deep sense of contentment as her eyes fluttered shut.

Meanwhile, Paul and Jarred lingered in the milk house, not far from where Maddie was sleeping. They hadn't told her, but they weren't planning on leaving her completely alone. They'd stay nearby, just in case.

"She's too stubborn for her own good," Paul muttered. Jarred smirked. "That's what makes her Maddie."

They eventually got restless and climbed onto the rafters in the barn, stretching out above the sleeping cows, talking about everything.

The night was warm, the farm quiet except for the occasional low moo of a restless cow.

"Alright, Jar. We gotta get some shut eye, as Grandma would say. See ya in the morning."

"G'night, Paul."

A flicker of light caught Jarred's half-closed eyes. He blinked, exhaustion pulling at him, but something felt off.

Then he saw the flames.

Bright orange embers flickered against the darkness, licking hungrily at the wooden beams near the barn's entrance.

Jarred bolted upright. His legs screamed in protest as he jumped down from the rafters, but he barely registered the pain.

"PAUL! Call the fire station! The barn is on fire!"

Paul was already scrambling down, his face flushing as he sprinted toward the house to grab a phone.

Heat roared against Jarred's skin. The flames spread fast, consuming dry hay and wood, curling up the barn walls like hungry fingers.

And then his stomach dropped.

Maddie.

She was still inside.

Through the thick smoke, he could barely make out her motionless figure beside Gem-Sparkles. The red and white

Holstein let out a deep, hoarse bellow, standing protectively over Maddie as if she understood the danger.

Jarred didn't hesitate.

He lunged through the fire, his body screaming in protest as flames scorched his skin. Smoke clawed at his throat, making each breath agonizing, but he kept going.

The barn groaned around him, embers falling like molten raindrops. His vision blurred, the world a mix of burning reds and suffocating blacks.

God, please. Just let me get to her.

Jumping through a circle of flames, Jarred dropped to his knees beside Maddie. Her jeans smoldered at the edges, the fire hungrily inching closer. He ripped off his shirt, slapping at the flames before they could take hold.

His lungs burned. His body shook. But he didn't stop. He couldn't. Adrenaline pumped through every cell in Jarred's body.

Gem-Sparkles let out another mournful sound, nudging Maddie's still form with her nose. The firelight reflected in the cow's dark eyes, and for a brief moment, Jarred swore he saw understanding there.

He knew the cow wouldn't make it.

He grabbed Maddie under her arms and threw her as close to the door as he could manage with the last of his strength. The fire roared louder, beams snapping overhead.

God, please. Let Paul find Maddie in time.

He staggered toward the open barn doors himself. Just a few more steps.

A deafening crack split the air.

Jarred looked up. Before the world tilted sideways, a beam collapsed above him.

And then darkness.

Cinders of Yesterday

The steady *beep ... beep ... beep* of a heart monitor pulled Jarred from the darkness. His body felt heavy, as if it were pinned beneath a thousand pounds of stone.

Something itched against his face, tight and unmoving, and his throat was raw, each shallow breath scraping like sandpaper. He swallowed, but his mouth was too dry.

He shifted slightly, the thin hospital sheets rustling against his aching body. A faint noise to his right made him turn his head. He tried to open his eyes, but the world remained dark.

Before he could say anything, a familiar voice stopped him.

"Don't speak, Jarred." His mother's voice was soft but trembling. She was close. "You need to rest your voice. The doctors don't want you straining your lungs after inhaling so much smoke."

Her fingers brushed lightly over his bandaged hand, and

he squeezed them weakly.

"Oh, baby," Dara whispered. "You were so brave." Her voice caught, and for a moment, she didn't speak. "I love you so much."

Jarred swallowed again, trying to push through the fog in his brain. He wanted to ask what happened, but the words wouldn't come.

Dara must have sensed his confusion. "I'm going to ask you a few questions now. Just nod for yes and shake your head for no, okay?"

He nodded, barely.

"Do you remember what happened?"

Jarred hesitated, then slowly shook his head.

A long pause. Then, his mother spoke again, quieter this time. "You saved your sister's life."

His chest tightened.

"Maddie's alive," Dara reassured him quickly. "She's in surgery right now. She's strong, just like you. But ... she was hurt, sweetheart. They believe that there was too much optic nerve damage due to severe burns."

The heart monitor beeped faster.

"Paul got back to you and Maddie soon after you must have caught on fire because you were in flames when he got to you," Dara choked.

Jarred could hear the pain in her voice.

"You were lying on the floor ... unconscious ... on fire." Her voice cracked. "Paul put the flames out as fast as he could. He dragged you out before the barn collapsed completely. Baby ... Gem-Sparkles blocked you from most of the fire. She saved you." Dara began to cry.

The memory was fuzzy, but through the haze, Jarred could almost feel the way Gem-Sparkles had stood over Maddie, shielding her. The sound of her hoarse, desperate moo before the fire swallowed her.

A single tear slipped down his cheek.

Dara's voice grew softer. "Your dad and grandparents are here. The doctors say you'll need to stay in the hospital for at least a month because of the burns. I know it's a lot to take in, but we'll get through this together. Your bandages will come off in a few weeks." She hesitated. "And Maddie ... well, we just have to keep praying."

Jarred lay still, feeling like he'd been hit by a freight train. Maddie was alive.

Gem-Sparkles was gone.

And nothing would ever be the same again. The next three weeks crawled by. Jarred had too much time to think.

His body ached, but the worst pain wasn't physical. Maddie was still in a coma. His mother spent her time bouncing between their hospital rooms while his dad and Paul kept the farm running.

For hours, he lay alone, trapped in his thoughts.

He couldn't remember everything from the fire, but flashes haunted him. The heat. The smoke clawed at his brain. The deafening crack of the barn collapsing.

The feeling of helplessness.

When the day finally came to remove the bandages, a strange mixture of relief and dread settled in his chest.

Dr. Lapel, the towering former football player turned doctor, stood at his bedside. "Alright, Jarred. Here we go."

Dara stood beside him, her hand resting gently on his bed.

The bandages loosened, layer by layer, until finally, cool air brushed against his skin.

His mother exhaled, tears shimmering in her eyes. "Oh, baby."

Dr. Lapel nodded. "Your wounds are healing nicely. That's a blessing."

Dara smiled, wiping her eyes. "Now that your hands are no longer wrapped, I'll get you a pen and paper so you can communicate easier."

Jarred nodded weakly. His fingers trembled as he took the pen a few moments later, scribbling on the notepad.

Mom, may I look in the mirror?

Ow. These burned hands of mine are no good, Jarred thought.

Dara hesitated. "Of course, sweetheart." She reached into her purse, pulling out a small hand mirror.

Jarred shook his head.

No. A full-sized mirror. I need to see everything.

A thick silence filled the room.

Dara's lips parted slightly, as if to protest, but she stopped herself. "Okay," she whispered.

Stacy, his nurse, left to find one. As they waited, Dara sat on the edge of the bed. "Honey," she began gently, "you were burned. Badly. There were three skin grafts. And ..." She hesitated, looking away.

Jarred gripped the pen tighter.

What are you not telling me?

Her voice was barely above a whisper. "You may never walk without assistance again."

His breath stalled.

Before he could process the words, Stacy returned, rolling in a full-length mirror.

With Dr. Lapel and Stacy supporting his waist, Jarred was carefully lifted from the bed. His muscles screamed in anguish, but he barely noticed.

He stared in the mirror. And froze.

Scars twisted across his skin, angry and red, marring his once-strong frame. The burns had stripped away the familiarity of his own reflection.

It was like looking at a stranger.

He didn't cry. He couldn't.

He just stood there, numb, staring into the eyes of a boy he no longer recognized.

"We're all here for you," Dara said softly.

Jarred blinked. His fingers curled around the notepad again, writing with slow, deliberate strokes.

I want to see Maddie.

Dara sighed. "Honey, she's still in a coma. You don't have to see her like that."

Jarred's grip on the pen tightened.

Stop. I can handle it. Take me to her.

His mother hesitated, reading the unshakable determination in his eyes.

Finally, she nodded. "Okay."

Turning to Dr. Lapel, she added, “Thank you for helping him stand. If you could assist him into the wheelchair, Stacy and I will take it from here.”

Dr. Lapel nodded, gently guiding Jarred down into the chair.

As Dara wheeled him toward Maddie’s room, he felt the weight of reality settle deep in his bones.

Nothing would ever be the same.

Jarred

When they arrived at Maddie's hospital room, silence suffocated every inch of the space. The atmosphere was still, as everyone stepped aside when Stacy wheeled Jarred in. There she lay. Jarred studied his sister's face, wrapped in white wraps, hiding open burn wounds. In the hospital bed, she looked so tiny and frail and ... lifeless.

Jarred asked everyone to leave for a while so he could be alone with her.

In an oversized, sterile, plain-white hospital room, Jarred sat propped up by a whole slew of support bed wedges and pillows on the edge of Maddie's bedside. Even though the room seemed plain, a corner full of bouquets hid in the corner. A bouquet full of sunflowers from the Lerian family stuck out from the crowd.

James had gone out to their sunflower field and picked the prettiest-looking sunflowers, knowing they were Maddie's favorite. He remembered how, during one of their dirt bike adventures, Maddie had spotted a lone sunflower and insisted on stopping to pick it. Maddie had a way of brightening everything around her, just like a sunflower. Liza and the twins had added a few colorful flowers from the meadow to the sunflowers so the bouquet would look uniquely exquisite.

Jarred looked through the window while continuing to sit on Maddie's bed, seeing hundreds of smokestacks from the overcrowded city buildings. Jarred sighed. He missed the brisk morning air, which he had only experienced on the farm. He missed the dandelions' dander floating up his nose. He missed his mom's homemade peach pie made from peaches picked off the tree in their front yard. He even missed the long hours he spent studying for his medical exams.

His medical exams.

Ever since he was a child, Jarred had his heart set on being a doctor. Watching his father tend to the animals all his life taught Jarred how important good health was in animals' and people's lives. But now, that dream felt impossibly distant. He couldn't walk, let alone speak freely. He was no longer the healer; he needed to heal himself. He took a moment to pray:

God ... I don't even know where to start. I don't know if I should be angry or thankful. I'm alive, but what kind of life is this? I can't walk. My vocal cords are sizzled. They say the burns were so severe that, even if I heal, life won't be the same. I won't be the same. I hear them whispering when they think I'm asleep, about surgeries, therapy, long-term care. But none of it matters, does it? Because Maddie ...

I can't stop looking at her, God. She's right there, so still. Too still. The machines should be coaxing her awake, but she's not waking up. She's not laughing. She isn't even sloshing around the usual bucketful of sunshine that she carries around with her everywhere. She's just … there. And I don't know if she's coming *back*.

Why, God? Why her? Why me? I would do anything if it meant I could hear her voice again. But I can't do anything. I can't even get out of this bed without assistance. I should have done something, anything, but I wasn't strong enough, wasn't fast enough. And now? Now I'm stuck here, useless, while she fights for her life.

I want to trust You. I really do. But if You have a plan for all this, I don't see it. All I see is pain. And this just stinks. All I feel is loss. And I don't know how to keep going like this. Help me. I … am … weak.

Jarred pleaded with God for a few minutes. Then he wept, mourning his old life.

A saltiness lingered in the back of Jarred's throat from some medication Stacy gave him that morning. He smelled the sterile air. He felt as if his life had lost its purpose. Jarred gently took his sister's hand in his. Ignoring the strain on his throat, he spoke.

"Maddie," he said softly in a hoarse voice. "I hope you can hear me, and I also know you can't respond yet, which is okay. I want to remind you that I'm here for you. I'm in rough shape, but I'll try to get better if you start your recovery with me. The past can't be changed, so we need to move forward. You're my only sister and a dear friend, so you need to get better. This is the first time I'm seeing you since the fire, you know, so bear with me because I'm still trying to wrap my head around everything."

Jarred paused, a little out of breath.

"Well, you see. You were sleeping when I woke up from the rafters. To the best of my recollection, I went down to the barn where you were sleeping with Gem-Sparkles, and sparks shot up from the floorboards, burning my legs. I had a tough time getting the barn door open to find you, but I finally managed to get to you. Gem-Sparkles saved both of our lives that night. I don't remember much after that, but I do remember hearing a faint voice saying, 'Let's get outta here before it's too late.' I'm not sure if it was my imagination or what, but that's what I heard. Maybe that voice was the Spirit giving me the strength to keep going. Fires do happen during the dry season, as you know, so maybe that's what happened. I just want you to get better."

He then prayed over her:

Dear God,

Please, dear Lord, take care of my sister. She means an awful lot to our family and many others. Thank you for waking me up in time to get her out of the flames, and thank you for waking Paul up in time to save both her and me. I am forever grateful for that. In Your time, please give me the strength to overcome the obstacles that I will face in my life.

In Jesus' name, Amen.

At that moment, Maddie's pinky finger twitched slightly in his hand. It was a subtle but undeniable movement.

"Stacy! Come here, quickly!" Jarred yelled for the nurse.

"What is it? Don't yell! You shouldn't be talking yet. Here's your pen and paper." Stacy was stunned that Jarred talked.

"Screw that. I know my voice is still sore, but I wanted to say that Maddie just moved her hand! It was an infinitesimal movement, but it was a movement nonetheless."

"Are you sure? She hasn't moved a muscle since the fire," Stacy replied.

"Yes. I know that, but I really did feel her move," Jarred insisted firmly.

"Check her vitals, Stacy. Please," Dara said, rushing into the room. "I need to know for sure if my baby girl is getting better."

Stacy immediately grabbed the equipment and checked. "I'm getting something. Her breathing is becoming more regular. Doctor, Doctor! Come in here quickly," she shouted excitedly.

After a few excruciatingly drawn-out minutes, Dr. Lapel told Dara that her daughter was coming around but might not be as she was before the fire.

Dara immediately called her husband to share the miraculous news.

☼

When Maddie awoke a week later, her loved ones' worst fear had come true. She was blind.

"Mama, I can't see you!" Maddie screamed.

Taking her daughter in her arms, Dara held her close. "Hold me, Mama. Never let go."

"I'm here, sweetheart. I'm here."

Maddie was asked a series of questions when she calmed down. She could answer most of them. She remembered her name and recalled falling asleep while talking to her beloved cow, Gem-Sparkles.

"I miss her, Jarred," Maddie said weakly. "She helped me fall asleep that night because I kept tossing and turning, missing Mom and Dad."

However, Maddie couldn't remember the fire or anything that happened afterward. Still, she mentioned hearing bits of what Jarred had said when he sat by her bed and cried the week before.

She was in shock when she heard what had happened. Her precious cow died. Her prized Holstein was devoured by the fire and lost in the flames.

As the weeks passed, Maddie and Jarred started going to physical therapy. Three months after the fire, both Maddie and Jarred were back home and getting better day by day. Maddie would sit on the sofa in the living room for hours and rock back and forth, humming to herself. Jarred began studying for medical exams again, along with doing at-home exercises throughout the day.

Seven months after the night of the fire, Jarred could walk with just the help of a cane. Maddie could walk several feet with the help of leg braces and a walker.

They were both eager to return to school in September. It took them nearly a year to recover. During that time, Mrs. McDowe implemented a homeschool program that Maddie, in particular, disliked.

Even though Jarred had accepted himself after the fire,

he feared how others would look at him. Would they still see him as the "future doctor of Marinette, Wisconsin," or would they pity him? He wasn't sure how he was going to get from class to class without others running into him, let alone how he would keep up with the boys in the field. He knew something, though. He knew he needed to take everything one step at a time.

Back to the Blackboard

The first day back at school was worse than Jarred had expected.

This was the first time since the fire that Paul drove to school with Jarred and Maddie. Though they sat in silence for most of the drive, Paul was glad to not have had to drive alone.

When Paul put the rusty, red Volkswagen in park, Jarred hesitated before opening the car door and stepping out. Paul went to the trunk and grabbed his and Maddie's backpacks before going to Maddie's door to help guide her to the school. "Come on, Mads. I'll be your eyes the whole way there."

"Thanks, Paul. Thankful for you. Go slow. Even though we walked the path yesterday to familiarize myself with the layout, I'm uneasy."

"Sounds good. We'll go slow."

The school felt both familiar and foreign, like a place Jarred should know but couldn't quite recognize. The last time he'd walked these halls, he hadn't needed a cane. His body hadn't been covered in healing burns. His name hadn't been whispered like a ghost story.

Now, as he walked through the hallway, it felt like every pair of eyes was on him.

The usual morning buzz of conversation quieted as he passed. Students whispered behind their hands. Others openly stared. It was like walking in slow motion, his presence sucking the life out of the hallway.

And then, all at once, the questions bellowed in like a gust of wind.

"What happened to you?" "How's your sister?" "Are you back to working on the farm?" "Did it hurt?" "I can't believe you survived that fire, man! What a cool story of heroism." "Do you feel like an old person using a cane?"

His head spun. The voices were overlapping, growing louder, feeding off each other. Jarred raised a hand, trying to quiet them. "Please stop," he said, but his voice barely carried over the noise. His pulse quickened, and the fluorescent lights above him buzzed.

"I mean, who in their right mind would jump into a fire for their sister? Come on, man. Just admit it. You didn't want to let her get all the attention."

Jarred's breath jerked to a stop for a split second. His vision blurred at the edges. His stomach twisted, and suddenly, the hallway felt too small. His lungs tightened as though the smoke from that night had found him all over again.

"Jarred!" A hand clamped onto his arm. It was his best friend, Nate. "Breathe, man. You're alright."

Jarred sucked in air, forcing himself to focus. Slowly, the dizziness passed. Teachers swooped in, dispersing the crowd, but the damage was done. The words hung in the air.

Who would risk their life for their sister? Come on. Who said that? Jarred thought to himself.

The fire had been ruled an accident. Just bad luck ... an electrical issue ... maybe a spark in the hay. Fires happened on farms all the time.

But if that was true, why did something about it still feel so wrong?

Unveiled Secrets

Jarred and his dad sat at the table alone.

"Dad? Can I have a man-to-man conversation with you?"

His dad rubbed a hand over his face. "Anything, son. About what?" He put down the newspaper he was reading.

"Was there an investigation done after the fire?"

Tyler nodded and stood up, grabbing a folder out of the filing cabinet in the corner of the living room that was connected to the kitchen. He set it down on the table. "I have been waiting for you to ask. Here's what we know," he said, flipping it open.

Jarred stared at the contents.

Photos. Notes. Copies of police reports.

His dad pointed to a grainy photo taken from a security camera at the gas station across the road. A dark sedan, headlights cutting through the night. "This car headed up the driveway toward the barns."

“This was taken at 12:43 a.m.,” his dad said. “The night of the fire.”

Jarred’s throat tightened.

“This same car was captured again on these security tapes about the time when Paul dialed 911. The sheriff tried to enhance the footage, but the plates were indecipherable. The car hasn’t been identified.”

Jarred’s hands clenched. “But someone was inside. Someone who knew what was about to happen.”

His dad nodded grimly. “That’s what I believe.” “Did they find anything else?”

His father exhaled slowly. “There was no clear evidence of arson. If someone set that fire, they knew exactly how to make it look like an accident.”

“So what now?” Jarred asked.

His dad leaned forward, eyes serious. “Now, we wait. We keep listening. Watching. If someone was behind this, they’ll slip up.”

Jarred nodded, but inside, he knew waiting wasn’t enough. Someone had been there that night.

And he wasn’t going to stop searching until he found out who.

An Unsettling Familiarity

A week had passed since Jarred first saw the security footage. A week since that dark sedan had etched itself into his mind.

Now, standing in the school parking lot waiting for Nate, Jarred's stomach twisted as something too familiar slid into view.

A dark sedan rolled up to the curb, its headlights cutting through the morning fog.

The back door opened. Macy and JoAnna Pewasta stepped out.

Jarred's jaw tensed. The sheriff had dismissed them, saying there wasn't enough to pursue. But he couldn't shake the gut feeling that the Pewasta girls had at least something to do with the fire.

And then, just like she'd been waiting for him, JoAnna found him in the hallway. Again.

She'd been doing this all week, floating into his world like a shadow. Friendly, warm ... casual.

"Hey," she said. "I was hoping I'd see you."

Jarred closed his locker slowly, studying her. "G'morning."

She leaned against the row of lockers beside him, twirling the strap of her bag. "How's everything? You look ... better and better."

He offered a small nod. "Getting there."

She hesitated, her gaze flickering past him toward the front doors. "We got here a little late. Traffic at the gas station was nuts."

Jarred stilled.

"In our little town? What gas station?" he asked, his voice low but gentle.

JoAnna blinked. "Uh ... the one a few miles from Olive's. That little family restaurant."

Jarred tilted his head slightly. "The one across from my family's farm?"

She caught herself. "Oh, no. A different one, I think." But it was too late.

His eyes didn't leave hers. "You know, I saw a car like yours on some footage. Near my place. Same night as the fire."

Her smile faltered.

"I should get to class," she said quickly, tucking some hair behind her ear. "Catch you later?"

Jarred didn't answer. He just watched her walk away,

heart thudding. She'd slipped.

Now he just needed to figure out how deep the truth went.

☼

The next afternoon, JoAnna was waiting for Jarred near the courtyard benches, where most kids avoided lingering in the cold.

Jarred walked up slowly, hands in his pockets, gaze locked on hers. "We need to talk."

JoAnna gave him a wary smile. "You sound serious." "I am."

She crossed her arms, trying to play it cool. "So then, talk."

"You were at the gas station that night," Jarred said evenly. "The one near my house."

Her expression didn't change, but her shoulders tightened. "Maybe. Why does it matter?"

"You didn't fill up. You pulled in, waited, then left. Like you were checking something."

JoAnna's lips parted for a second, then pressed shut.

Then she gave a light, disbelieving laugh. "Are you accusing me of something?"

"I'm saying the timing's weird. And your car matches the sedan in the footage."

Silence.

Then, there was a quiet shift. JoAnna's shoulders slumped just slightly. "You ever feel like no matter what you do, it doesn't matter?"

The question puzzled him. "What?"

She glanced down at her boots. "Like ... you could be perfect. You could follow all the rules. And still, someone else gets to decide what your life looks like."

Jarred studied her. "What are you trying to say?" She didn't answer directly.

Instead, she looked up, her voice gentler now. "I wasn't like those girls who fawned over you, Jarred. I knew better. I just hoped you would glance my way. But Macy? She hated how you saw people. The way you noticed the things everyone else missed."

He felt his breath catch.

"And Maddie was just like you," she added, quieter. "That's what really got under Macy's skin."

His heart pounded. "Why?"

JoAnna's jaw tightened. "Because Maddie had what we didn't. A real home. Brothers who doted upon their sister."

She looked away. "Macy never had that." Jarred stayed still. "So she set a fire?" JoAnna said nothing.

"Did you help her?" he pressed.

A flicker of fear shone in her eyes.

She shrugged, too slow, too casual. "If you really thought that, wouldn't the cops already be involved?"

"I don't accuse people without evidence," Jarred said calmly. "But I'm looking. We need ... "

JoAnna's smirk faltered.

"We've already made our choices," she said after a long pause. Then she turned and walked away.

And Jarred was left staring after her, the weight of her words pressing down like smoke coming into view.

Breaking the Silence

The next day, Jarred felt wired.

He sat through his classes, barely hearing a word the teachers said, his mind locked on the follow-up meeting he had set up with JoAnna after school.

By the time the last bell rang, he was already out the door, making his way to the back of the school where the buses idled. JoAnna was waiting, arms crossed, weight shifted onto one leg like she was bored.

But he knew better.

"Alright, Jarred," she said as soon as he got close. "I'm here. What do you want?"

Jarred didn't answer immediately. He just really studied her.

The way her hands flexed slightly at her sides. The way her jaw was tight, like she was already on the defensive.

She knew what this was about.

"Macy started the fire," he said, keeping his voice steady. "You were with her. Maybe you didn't light the match, but you knew what she was going to do."

JoAnna's gaze flickered, but she scoffed. "You don't have proof of that."

Jarred took a slow breath. "Not yet."

She stiffened.

He took a step closer, lowering his voice. "But I will."

For a moment, JoAnna said nothing. Then, she rolled her shoulders back, forcing a smirk. "Let's say Macy was involved, hypothetically. What would you do? Run to the cops?"

"Yes," Jarred said immediately. That seemed to catch her off guard.

Her face twitched, then settled into something unreadable. "You really think that'll change anything?"

Jarred clenched his jaw. "It'll change everything."

JoAnna let out a breath, shaking her head. "You don't get it."

"No, you don't get it," he snapped. "My family almost died. My sister—" He exhaled sharply, forcing himself to calm down. "Macy did this. And you helped her."

JoAnna's fingers curled into fists. She opened her mouth as if to speak, but then closed it, turning her head slightly.

Something passed over her face. Regret.

Guilt.

Something raw.

The walls of her heart crumbled a little more.

"I didn't think it would go that far," she murmured,

almost too quiet to hear. "Macy just ... wanted to scare you. Make you understand what it's like to lose something."

Jarred's stomach twisted. "By setting a fire?" JoAnna flinched.

Jarred pressed on. "What happened that night?" She hesitated.

"I drove her," JoAnna admitted. "She told me she just wanted to freak you guys out. A small fire. Something that would make a point. But when I realized she wasn't putting it out, it was already too late."

Jarred's hands curled into clenched fists. "You could have stopped her."

JoAnna's face hardened. "Do you know what it's like to have someone control you? To know that if you step out of line, you'll be next?"

Jarred narrowed his eyes. "Macy threatened you?"

JoAnna laughed bitterly. "Not directly. But she didn't have to."

For a second, Jarred saw the exhaustion, the fear she'd been carrying.

But it didn't change the truth.

"You need to go to the police," he said.

JoAnna snapped her head up. "No."

"Yes," he pressed. "You were involved, but you weren't the one who started it. If you go willingly, if you tell them what really happened, it'll be better for you."

She shook her head, stepping back. "You don't understand. If I say anything, Macy will—" She cut herself off.

Jarred took a step forward. “She’ll what?” JoAnna swallowed. “It doesn’t matter.”

“Yes, it does.” His voice was softer now. “You don’t have to protect her.”

She laughed dryly. “You think I’m protecting her?” She gestured vaguely, her expression caught between frustration and something else. “I’m protecting myself.”

Jarred exhaled slowly. “Then let me help you.” Silence.

JoAnna looked away, something unreadable crossing her face.

Then, without another word, she turned and walked off, disappearing into the parking lot.

Jarred stood there, his heart pounding. She wasn’t going to the police. But oh, he certainly was.

The Call for Justice

Jarred sat on the porch steps, not realizing he was gripping his phone so tightly his knuckles turned white.

Paul sat next to him, arms crossed. “You sure about this?” “Yes.”

Paul nodded slowly. “Then do it.”

Jarred exhaled and called the police.

The line rang once. Twice. “Sheriff Ryan speaking. How may I help you?”

Jarred’s throat tightened, but he forced himself to speak. “It’s Jarred McDowe.”

There was a pause. “What can I do for you, son?”

Jarred glanced at Paul, who gave him a firm nod. “I have information about the fire.”

The silence on the other end stretched.

Then, the sheriff’s voice came back, sharper this time.

“Go on.” Jarred took a deep breath. “I know who did it.”

Thirty minutes later, Sheriff Ryan pulled into the driveway, his cruiser kicking up dust as it came to a stop.

Jarred and Paul met him halfway, their father stepping out onto the porch behind them.

The sheriff wasted no time. “Start from the beginning.”

Jarred took a steadying breath and told him everything he knew.

The security footage. The gas station. The dark sedan. JoAnna’s half-confession.

As he spoke, the sheriff’s expression darkened.

When Jarred finished, Sheriff Ryan let out a heavy sigh and rubbed his jaw. “You’re telling me JoAnna Pewasta admitted to being involved?”

“She didn’t admit it outright,” Jarred slunk backward. “But she all but confirmed it. She drove Macy. She knew what was happening.”

The sheriff was quiet for a moment. Then, he nodded. “Alright. I’ll take it from here.”

Jarred’s pulse pounded. “What does that mean?” “It means I’ll be paying the Pewastas a visit.” Jarred swallowed. “And if she denies everything?”

Sheriff Ryan exhaled through his nose. “Then we keep digging.” Paul shifted beside him. “But what if she confesses?”

The sheriff’s face was unreadable. “Then Macy Pewasta’s looking at a felony charge.”

Jarred’s chest hardened.

This wasn’t just an idea anymore. The truth was finally coming out.

And the Pewasta sisters were about to face the consequences.

Truth

The Pewastas' house sat at the end of a long, gravel road, the once-white paint peeling under years of neglect. Sheriff Ryan pulled up slowly, his tires crunching over loose stones.

He stepped out, strode up to the front door, and knocked firmly, waiting.

There was a long pause. Then the door cracked open, and JoAnna appeared. Her face paled the second she saw him.

"Is your mother home?" the sheriff asked.

JoAnna hesitated before shaking her head. "No." "Macy?"

JoAnna swallowed hard, contemplating what to say.

"Macy!" The sheriff's voice carried through the doorway. Silence.

Then, a shuffling noise. Moments later, Macy appeared behind her sister, arms crossed, chin tilted defiantly. "What do you want?"

Sheriff Ryan's eyes were sharp. "We need to talk about the fire."

Macy's expression didn't change. "We don't know anything about that."

JoAnna flinched.

Sheriff Ryan stepped closer. "That so?" He folded his arms. "Funny, because I've got someone who says otherwise."

Macy's jaw tightened. "Who?" "Your sister."

JoAnna stiffened beside her, eyes darting to the ground. Macy scoffed. "She wouldn't."

"She did," Sheriff Ryan said evenly. "And if you want my advice, you'd better start talking before this gets worse for you."

Macy glared at her sister. "You said nothing, right?" JoAnna didn't answer.

That silence said everything.

Macy's face twisted. "You're a coward."

JoAnna lifted her head, something shifting in her expression. For the first time, she looked done.

"No, Macy," she murmured. "I just don't want to be like the old us anymore."

Macy's eyes flashed, but before she could respond, Sheriff Ryan interrupted. "Enough." He turned to JoAnna. "Are you willing to testify to what you told Jarred?"

JoAnna hesitated.

Then, slowly, she nodded.

Macy let out a bitter laugh. "Unbelievable." She turned away, shaking her head. "I did you a favor, Jo. You just don't see it yet."

"A favor?" JoAnna snapped. "You set a fire, Macy! You could have killed people!"

Macy rolled her eyes. "I wasn't trying to kill anyone."

"That's not how the law sees it," Sheriff Ryan said firmly.

Macy went still.

JoAnna exhaled sharply. "I'm done covering for you." She turned to Sheriff Ryan, voice quiet but steady. "Macy set a fire, and I accompanied her."

It was over. The truth was finally out.

McDowe v. Pewasta

The judge's gavel struck the wooden block, sending a crisp crack through the courtroom.

"All rise," the bailiff announced as Judge Lakeland took his seat at the bench. His sharp gaze swept across the room before he nodded for everyone to sit.

Jarred settled into his chair, the weight of the moment pressing against his ribs. His father sat beside him, rigid. Paul's fists were clenched on his lap, his jaw tight.

Across the aisle, JoAnna sat stiff-backed, her hands gripping the edge of the table. Macy, by contrast, slouched in her chair, arms crossed, her expression vacant. But Jarred knew her well enough by now to recognize what was beneath it: resentment.

Judge Lakeland adjusted his glasses and cleared his throat. "We are here today to hear the case of the *State of Wisconsin v. Macy and JoAnna Pewasta*, concerning the charges of arson and reckless endangerment."

A murmur rippled through the courtroom, quickly silenced by another bang of the gavel.

"The prosecution may begin."

A woman stood, sharp and composed in a navy suit. "Thank you, Your Honor." She turned to the jury. "Ladies and gentlemen, what we have here is a deliberate act of destruction. Macy Pewasta planned and executed the burning of the McDowe family's barn, a crime that not only caused thousands of dollars in damages but also endangered the lives of livestock and the McDowe family. JoAnna Pewasta, though not the one who lit the fire, played an active role in enabling this crime. Today, we will prove beyond a reasonable doubt that these actions were not accidental but intentional, driven by jealousy, resentment, and a reckless disregard for human life."

She stepped back, nodding toward the defense table. "The facts will speak for themselves."

The defense attorney, a wiry man with graying hair, stood next. His voice was smooth, but his gaze was sharp. "Your Honor, ladies and gentlemen of the jury, what happened that night was a mistake, an act of misguided emotion rather than true malice. Macy Pewasta did not intend to cause harm to Maddie and Jarred. She did not seek destruction for the sake of it. Instead, she acted out of deep emotional distress, fueled by personal struggles that we will present to you in detail. We ask that you consider the full picture before passing judgment."

Jarred felt Paul shift beside him, and he knew his brother was biting back a scoff. A mistake? That was their defense?

The judge nodded. "The prosecution may call its first witness."

The attorney turned. "We call Jarred McDowe to the stand."

Jarred's heart kicked against his ribs. This was it.

He stood, stepping forward, his hands cold as he was sworn in.

Once seated, the prosecutor approached. "Jarred, can you describe the events of the night of the fire?"

He took a breath. "I was coming home late from a friend's place when I saw the glow in the distance. By the time I got there, the barn was already in flames. Paul called 911 and tried to get the animals out, but ..." He swallowed. "It was too late for some."

"Did you see anyone near the barn?"

"No. But later, I found out that a dark sedan had been seen in the area before the fire started. The same car the Pewasta sisters drive."

The prosecutor nodded. "Did you confront JoAnna about this?"

"Yes. At school, a week after I saw the video footage."

"What did she say?"

Jarred hesitated, his eyes flickering to JoAnna. She was already looking at him, her expression unreadable.

"She tried to avoid answering at first. But eventually, she told me that Macy had started the fire. That she had driven her there."

A murmur spread through the courtroom.

"No further questions."

The defense lawyer stood, buttoning his suit jacket.

"Jarred, you and your sister Maddie are well-liked at school, correct?"

Jarred frowned. "I guess so."

"And would you say Macy Pewasta struggled socially?"

He stiffened. "What does that have to do with anything?"

The lawyer smiled slightly. "Just answer the question."

"Yes."

The attorney nodded as if that was exactly what he expected. "And isn't it true that your family has had issues with the Pewasta family in the past?"

Jarred hesitated. "We ... don't really interact much."

"But your father had arguments with their mother, did he not?"

Jarred glanced at his dad, whose jaw was set like stone. "I guess."

The lawyer turned to the jury. "Tension existed long before this fire, ladies and gentlemen. And that tension, those divisions, play into how we view this situation." He turned back to Jarred. "That's all."

Jarred exhaled, standing as the judge dismissed him. He returned to his seat, pulse still hammering.

JoAnna was called next.

She walked to the stand with slow, careful steps. Once sworn in, the prosecutor approached. "JoAnna, tell us what happened the night of the fire."

Her hands gripped the wooden stand. "Macy told me she wanted to do something. Something that would make the McDowes see how good they had it. I didn't ask for details. I just drove her."

"Did you know she was planning to start a fire?"

She hesitated.

Then, she said softly, "I knew she wanted to do something drastic." "But you didn't stop her?"

"No."

A pang of guilt flashed across her face.

"Why?"

JoAnna closed her eyes briefly, then met the prosecutor's gaze. "Because I was scared of her."

A collective hush fell over the courtroom.

"She has a temper," JoAnna admitted. "And she's the only person I have. I didn't want to lose her."

The defense lawyer stood. "JoAnna, isn't it true that you were under immense emotional stress when you gave your statement?"

She frowned. "What?"

"You were emotional, correct? Scared?" "Yes, but—"

"Is it possible that in your distress, you misunderstood Macy's intentions? That she never actually told you she was going to start a fire?"

JoAnna stiffened. "I plead the fifth."

The lawyer tilted his head. "Or is that just what you believe now that you're here, under pressure, being forced to testify against your own sister?"

JoAnna's hands clenched. "She did it."

The lawyer sighed, shaking his head. "No further questions."

The judge addressed Macy. "You may take the stand if you wish."

Macy hesitated. Then, she stood, her expression hard as she walked to the stand. After she was sworn in, the defense attorney approached first.

"Macy, did you set fire to the McDowe barn?"

She folded her arms, her jaw tight. "No."

From the other side of the room, Jarred felt his father tense beside him.

The lawyer nodded, as if expecting that response. "Then tell us. Where were you that night?"

Macy shrugged. "JoAnna and I were out driving. We stopped at the gas station for a little while."

"And at no point did you go near the McDowe property?"

"No."

The prosecutor stood now, stepping forward. "Macy, do you understand that lying under oath is a crime?"

Macy's eyes darkened. "I plead the fifth."

The prosecutor arched an eyebrow. "Your sister already told us that you planned this. She drove you to the farm. Are you saying she lied?"

Macy shot a look at JoAnna, whose head was bowed slightly. A flicker of something crossed her face before she schooled her expression. Was it betrayal?

"She doesn't know what she's talking about," Macy muttered.

The prosecutor let that hang in the air for a moment before speaking again. "Macy, you resented the McDowe family, didn't you?"

Macy's lips pressed into a gritted line.

"You were angry that they had the kind of home life you never did."

Macy's fists clenched in her lap.

The prosecutor leaned in slightly. "And that anger? It

built up until you needed a way to make them see how easy they had it. You thought burning down their barn would do that, didn't you?"

Macy snapped her head up, eyes flashing.

Jarred didn't move.

No one spoke.

Judge Lakeland's gaze was sharp. "Macy."

Macy's shoulders slumped. "I did it." Her voice wavered, and tears started dripping from her eyes, but she kept going. "I thought … I don't know what I thought. I just wanted them to feel what it was like to have something ripped away. To not have control over their own life. I didn't want anyone to get hurt. I swear, I didn't."

The prosecutor gave a slow nod, then turned to the judge. "No further questions."

The judge exhaled, looking down at the papers in front of him. "Court is adjourned until sentencing."

The gavel struck one last time.

As people rose from their seats, murmurs filled the room.

Jarred sat frozen, watching as Macy was led away in cuffs. She didn't fight it. Didn't even look back.

Beside him, Paul let out a breath. "She actually admitted it."

Their dad ran a hand down his face. "Yeah."

JoAnna stood near the defense table, arms wrapped around herself. She looked lost. Small.

For a moment, Jarred almost felt sorry for her. Almost.

Because no matter what, nothing would undo what had

already been done.

The courtroom was packed when the sentencing hearing began.

The weight of what had happened hung thick in the air: burned memories, ruined livelihoods, and a family still picking up the pieces.

Judge Lakeland settled in his chair, his expression unclear as he shuffled through documents. “Before we proceed with sentencing, is there anything either of the defendants would like to say?”

Macy remained silent, her gaze fixed on the table in front of her. JoAnna hesitated, then slowly stood.

“I just …” Her voice wavered as she gripped the podium. “I know I can’t take back what we did. I was wrong. I was weak. I went along with Macy because I thought it was the only way to be important to her.” Her voice cracked. “I should have stopped her. I should have spoken up. But I didn’t. And I have to live with that.”

She shook her head. “I don’t expect forgiveness. I don’t even deserve it.”

Silence followed. The McDowe family sat motionless, their expressions unreadable.

The judge folded his hands. “Very well. Let’s proceed with sentencing.”

The air in the courtroom grew heavier as he continued.

“Macy Pewasta, you are presumed not guilty, but that does not excuse the crime. You will serve one year in a juvenile detention facility, followed by three years of probation. You are required to attend mandatory mental health counseling, fire safety courses, and community service totaling one thousand hours. Any violation of these terms will result in additional sentencing."

A ripple of murmurs spread through the room. Macy clenched her jaw, nodding stiffly.

Judge Lakeland then turned his gaze to JoAnna.

"JoAnna Pewasta, you are found not guilty. While you did not set the fire yourself, you were complicit. You aided and abetted a felony and failed to take action when you had the chance to prevent harm. Because of this, the court sentences you to six months in a juvenile rehabilitation program, followed by two years of probation. Additionally, you will complete 750 hours of community service and attend court-mandated counseling."

JoAnna swallowed hard, nodding slowly.

The judge's voice softened just slightly. "Young ladies, the choices you made led to destruction, loss, and pain. This sentence is not just about punishment. It's about accountability. How you choose to move forward will determine whether this mistake defines you, or if you grow from it. The court hopes you will make the right choice."

He lifted the gavel. "Court is adjourned."

The bang of the gavel hitting the wooden block echoed through the room.

Macy's shoulders tensed as officers moved to escort her out. JoAnna stood still for a long moment before finally stepping away, her face unreadable.

From the back of the courtroom, Jarred let out a slow breath. Justice had been served.

But even as they left the courthouse, he knew this wasn't

over. Not really.

Because some wounds didn't heal with a sentence.

Scars always remain.

Mending Hearts

In the months that followed the trial, Maddie's nightmares worsened. She would awake from these horrible dreams in the middle of the night, screaming and shouting. "MOMMY! Mama!" Maddie gasped until her parents came rushing to her.

One night, as she had another episode, she screamed and said, "Mommy! It's real. It's all real. I can't see you, Mama. It's so dark."

Her mother came rushing from her room to comfort her and said, "Sweet girl. It'll be okay. You just woke up from a nightmare, is all. We're getting through this tough season of life together. Your dad's here too, darling. You are not alone."

"Here," Tyler sat on the side of Maddie's bed and took her hand, bringing it to his face. "Touch my face and know that I am here. I am your dad. You are loved, Maddie May. You are cherished. You are protected."

As the days passed, the pain and intensity of the dreams became so unbearable that Maddie started going to therapy. Her therapist, KellyAnn, learned what Maddie was passionate about and then built on that. She told Maddie that she wanted her to lean into her passion for painting and focus her attention on art, as it might free her mind, body, and soul from her haunting past.

KellyAnn knew what she was doing but feared her teachings wouldn't work. She knew every patient coped differently, and Maddie was no exception. Many of KellyAnn's patients loved her, but she lacked experience in dealing with blind patients. Maddie was her first. This was a challenge for her, but as a Christ follower, she believed God was there, granting Maddie with the strength to heal.

As their painting sessions began, KellyAnn started by positioning the colors on the color palette in an order Maddie was familiar with. This technique made it easier for Maddie to locate colors.

KellyAnn had green at twelve o'clock, blue at three o'clock, yellow at six o'clock, and brown at nine o'clock. Knowing which colors were at each location, Maddie began painting. KellyAnn didn't expect much, knowing it was Maddie's first painting after the accident. Maddie worked on this project for the next eight days.

During those eight days, peace flooded each vein in her body. The spark reignited her childhood passion. She knew that the sunshine that was once in her eyes had been rekindled within her soul, warming parts of herself she thought were lost forever. As she layered the paint onto the canvas, time became fluid. Minutes melted into hours, and the world outside ceased to exist. Each brushstroke was more than just pigment on fabric; it was a sort of healing, a silent conversation between her soul and God Himself.

She could feel the weight of the colors, their energy coursing through her fingertips. The green pulsed with life, whispering of renewal. The blue stretched wide, cool and endless, like the sky she used to stare at for hours. Yellow flickered like the last light given from the sunset. She felt hopeful again.

One fine evening, as Maddie's family prepared their supper, Dara noticed Maddie indulging in her painting.

"Maddie, darling. Please put your brush down and sit with us at dinner," Dara said, with slight hope in her voice.

"This couldn't be better timing. I'm just finishing up this wave in this cornfield. After that, I'll be at the dinner table. Thank you." Maddie responded as she smeared a stroke on the canvas. She ran her fingers lightly over the dried layers of paint, feeling the texture beneath her touch. It was a habit she quickly picked up after losing her sight, letting her hands guide her almost as much as her eyes used to. As the painting progressed, she listened as her mom described the colors she had already laid down. Bright yellow hues blended into dark amber, the deep blues bleeding into hints of violet. She nodded, letting her mom's words settle in her mind.

"You're welcome," Dara's mouth rested in a subtle smile, penetrating her lips, and she walked to the kitchen. Maddie quickly finished and brought her painting to the living room, where she passed it around to show everyone. Witnessing such elegance, all jaws nearly hit the ground.

"I painted a picture of where our woods begin. I remember vividly what it looked like, spending so much time in front of the window above the kitchen sink for many years. I tried my best to make it out how I see it in my head," Maddie said with a wide, sunny grin.

In the canvas frame, the trees not only made up the McDowes' woods but looked as if they were standing right before them. The grazing cows were the focus of the painting, but the cornfield on the left caught everyone's eye. Each stalk looked like it was being lifted off the canvas. Every tiny detail brought life to the painting, including a wee beetle landing on a single stalk.

After dinner, Tyler and Dara secretly went to the Lerians' house with Maddie's painting. Cari Lerian proposed sending it to an art fanatic, Eddie Kerleliquin, whom she knew from grade school. Tyler and Dara both agreed and handed over the painting.

Cari was a mother and ran a household, a candle business, and a bakery. She set everything up for her family and her business so they could all manage quite nicely without her for a while. Cari felt compelled to do something thoughtful for Dara's daughter, so she decided this was the perfect opportunity.

Cari left, kissing and hugging her family goodbye. They all kept this a secret from Maddie and the McDowe family. Although Mr. Kerleliquin didn't have much time, he met with Cari at a restaurant.

"It's been a long time, Ed," Cari said joyfully as she gave Eddie a side hug upon meeting him.

"Too long, doll," Eddie responded excitedly. "It surprised

me when my agent told me you had called. So, what do I owe the pleasure?"

"To my best friend's daughter," Cari responded, signaling to the waiter to come and take their order.

"Ahh. How is dear Dara doing? We haven't spoken in ages," Eddie asked inquisitively.

"I'm here on business, ol' buddy," Cari retorted.

Years back, Eddie went to school with both Dara and Cari. It was rumored that Eddie gushed over Dara once upon a time.

"Okay. I see you don't waste your time. What is it that you would like to propose?" Eddie inquired with great curiosity.

"One of Maddie McDowe's paintings. Her paintings are original. She paints pictures of her vision of the world. I have one of her paintings right here," Cari exclaimed, getting jumpier as the minutes ticked by.

Eddie's eyes lit up when Cari showed him the picture

"Whoa. I've never seen anything like this before. Now you say this is Dara's daughter. How long has she been painting like this?" Eddie responded as he took a deeper look at it.

"Well, she just started painting like this a few weeks ago. She became blind many months ago from a fire that almost cost her and her brothers' lives. She had to have a major life-saving surgery to live, but one of the surgery's side effects seemed to have left her blind. That's why I said she paints what she remembers or envisions the world to look like," Cari said with great pain in her eyes.

"Well, we can both agree that the girl's got talent,"

Eddie said, his gaze sweeping over the painting with an appraising, business-like curiosity. "But it's more than that. Her work isn't just art; it's like she's painting the weight of a memory, the echo of a voice, the texture of a feeling. Every detail adds another layer. Every color choice feels almost ... instinctive, like she's translating something the rest of us can't quite grasp with our eyes." He let out a deep breath, both impressed and intrigued. "How many paintings does she have, and at what price would she be selling them?"

"She only has four right now, plus she doesn't know that I'm here talking to you, so I don't know if she's willing to sell," Cari added assertively.

"Okay, you lost me a bit here. If that's the case, then why are you here?" asked Eddie.

"I'm here to find out if her paintings are as good as all of her loved ones think they are, without bias. I certainly think they're remarkable, but I love that child like she's my niece," Cari responded, her voice softening as a proud smile tugged at the corners of her lips, a glimmer of warmth and admiration dancing in her eyes.

"They certainly are good, to say the least, but I would have to see more to judge them truly. If you go home and tell Maddie that a professional art fanatic is intrigued by her work, and she begins working on paintings for a showcase, she might be looking at the next few years of her life as a painter. Give Dara my card so that she may read it to Maddie," Eddie said, leaning back slightly in his chair with a thoughtful nod, his fingers drumming lightly on the table as his eyes narrowed in quiet contemplation.

"Thank you, Eddie," Cari said, her voice warm and sincere.

Cari sang all the way home to her radio. She couldn't wait to tell Maddie the incredible news.

"Welcome home, dear," Mr. Lerian said.

"Mom, Mom! Did you tell famous people about Maddie's paintings?" Liza asked.

"Yes, darling. Would you like to go tell Maddie with me?"

"Oh, Mom. Of course." Liza grabbed her mom's arm and tugged her out the door as Mrs. Lerian shouted, "Liza, slow down. We should call her and ask if she's up for us to visit."

"I guess you're right."

Liza snatched her phone from her back pocket and called Maddie, who answered after three rings.

"Liza?"

"MADDIE!!!"

"Girl, my mom's got major news!" Liza put Maddie on speakerphone.

"Oh, cool! What is it, Mrs. Lerian?"

"Hi, Maddie. We were going to stop over and share the news with you in person, but we can tell you now. So I took one of your paintings to an old art exhibitionist I know, and he loved it so much he wanted to see more."

"What?! Oh, Mrs. Lerian! How can I ever thank you?"

"Sweetheart, you don't need to thank me."

Maddie agreed she needed time to think, but her ultimate

decision was yes. She would definitely let Mr. Kerleliquin look at them.

In the months that followed, Maddie began painting every day after school. She fell in love with the brush. Each evening, her nails, hair, and clothes were caked in a thin layer of paint. She painted rolling hills, mountaintops, country roads, and trees. Trees, in particular, fascinated her. Their solid, mighty presence seemed capable of taking over the world, yet they stood still, quiet. Maddie captured their stillness and serenity in her paintings, transporting viewers to a simpler time.

By the time Maddie was done, she had curated forty-six paintings for an art show in New York. Headlines across the nation told the story of the country girl who went blind in a fire but not in her mind. "The Most Magnificent Works of Art Seen by Man," the headlines proclaimed. Fame was a gift, but sometimes the McDowe family longed for their old life.

They often sat around their big oak table, sharing stories of "way back when." Those wonderful memories became a refuge in their suddenly eventful lives. Between running a farm and driving Maddie from state to state for art shows, they were mentally and physically exhausted. One night at the dinner table, Paul had an idea.

"We should have a game night! Let's invite Grandma, Grandpa, and the Lerians too. We all need a break, and this would be the perfect way to relax and have fun without worrying about tomorrow."

"Agreed. Let's have it this Sunday night!"

That Sunday, laughter and love echoed across the McDowe farm, audible even ten miles away through the popping of popcorn in the microwave. The sky was clear, with bright stars and a full moon shining overhead. It was a perfect night for family and friends to gather and share stories.

Paul started.

"Oh, I remember the day Jarred and I planned to run away with baby Maddie. She was about six months old. We packed our little yellow wagon with five peanut butter and jelly sandwiches and three vanilla puddings for Maddie. I guess we thought we'd survive the entire winter because we also packed our winter coats. We were ready to leave when Mom said, 'If you're running away, I need to run away with you.' Five-year-old me thought that made perfect sense, so the four of us set off. You let me lead, so we headed to the woods. We walked for two hours before deciding to go back. We ate some sandwiches for lunch, had pudding for dessert, and returned home for dinner."

"Mom, did you know we'd get tired and come back?" Jarred asked.

"Of course I did. I wasn't going to let my babies wander off alone."

"Ha-ha, or the time we dressed up the cows and put on a parade and talent show for you guys," Paul said, gesturing to their parents with a laugh.

"That was so darling," Dara replied, smiling.

"We even added Otis, a few goats, and a couple of chickens for the encore," Jarred chimed in with a laugh, recalling the chaotic but endearing scene.

"We were all so proud of that," Maddie exclaimed, her face lighting up at the memory. "We thought we were the greatest musketeers around!"

Paul leaned forward, his eyes gleaming as he remembered another unforgettable moment. "Do you all remember what happened at cousin Nala's wedding? We were on the golf course, trying our hand at some amateur golf. None of us were any good, but we were having a blast. Four-year-old Maddie was getting bored with the game, so Jarred and she went for a little walk near the tree line by the course to get some ants out of her pants. Out of nowhere, little four-year-old Maddie ended up face-to-face with a raccoon that had scampered out of the cover of the woods. The poor animal must have felt cornered or scared because it opened its mouth wide, as if it was ready to attack Maddie. It was terrifying!"

He paused for dramatic effect, then continued with growing enthusiasm. "Mom, I swear, you turned into Superwoman at that moment. One second, you were on the other side of the course by me and Dad, and the next, you were running faster than I'd ever seen anyone run, sweeping Maddie up into your arms and putting yourself between the coon and Jarred. And then, without even hesitating, you punched that raccoon square in the jaw! It was so crazy and cool at the same time. That coon couldn't run faster back into the safety of those trees. That was hands down the greatest wedding ever!" Paul finished, his voice brimming with excitement.

Dara chuckled softly, shaking her head as she responded, "Oh, I remember that so well. I just did what any good mother would do to protect her child. It wasn't anything extraordinary." Her sly smile suggested she knew just how extraordinary her actions had been, though.

Tyler, who had been quietly listening, added with a nervous laugh, "Yeah, that story definitely gets brought up every time I talk to Nala. She loves retelling it to anyone who'll listen. Honestly, I think that raccoon incident is more memorable to her than the wedding itself!"

"I have another fun story," Jarred said with a mischievous grin. "Remember Great-Grandma Missy's funeral?"

"How could we not remember? Don't tell this one. You tell it all the time, and it's embarrassing!" Paul groaned, his face already flushing at the thought.

"Oh, fine, I won't," Jarred replied with a dramatic sigh, though his smirk hinted he wasn't quite done yet.

"Remember when you missed the bus because you were upset about a test grade you got from Ms. Lepst, Maddie?" he asked, seamlessly shifting the subject.

"Yeah, I remember that," Maddie said, rolling her eyes at the memory. "I didn't like Ms. Lepst. She didn't know what she was talking about half the time. I supposedly got nine questions wrong, but later, when she reviewed my test with me, it turned out she had errors in her answer key! I mean, who does that?!"

Jarred chuckled. "Yeah, Paul and I were already on the bus when James noticed you weren't there. He bolted off the bus to find you."

"The bus didn't wait for either of you," Paul added. "James found you crying in the lunchroom. It started raining, and neither Mom nor Dad could pick you up because they were busy milking cows. So, you two had to wait outside the school for an hour. James' parents were both at work, so there was no one to help. You sat there until Cari finished her shift. When she finally arrived, you were wrapped up in James' sweatshirt, but you were still wet and shivering. James had blocked most of the rain for you, though, so you weren't completely soaked. James, on the other hand, was drenched and ended up sick in bed for a week." Paul gave James a friendly punch on the arm.

"Oh, that was awful," Dara chimed in, her voice filled with gratitude. "He had a severe case of pneumonia. We're definitely grateful to him for doing his best to keep our little girl healthy." She smiled warmly at James, her expression a mix of pride and appreciation.

Jarred's mischievous grin returned. "Well, I'm gonna tell the story, whether you like it or not. So, at Great-Grandma Missy's funeral, we each placed flowers on her casket. Paul was walking up to the casket, and as he stepped onto the fake green turf covering the hole, he slipped. Before anyone realized what had happened, Paul was under Great-Grandma Missy's casket, down in the grave!"

Jarred paused for effect, relishing the horrified and amused reactions. "Mom screamed like the world was ending, and Dad and Uncle Bernie sprinted to save him. Poor Mom was bawling her eyes out because they couldn't quite reach him. She was terrified the casket would fall on Paul and squish him flat like a bug. I was four and didn't really understand what was happening. I just wanted to go home. After twelve excruciatingly long minutes, Uncle Bernie finally managed to pull Paul out of the hole. And you know what? Paul still had Great-Grandma Missy's flowers clutched in his hand when he came out!"

Paul, his face now bright red, added, "I only remember it being really dark for a few minutes, and then suddenly, I was in Mom's arms. She was hugging me and smothering me with wet, sloppy kisses. At least, I think they were kisses, but it felt more like she was drooling on me!"

The group burst into laughter, and Maddie, gazing up at the stars, remarked softly, "It's such a beautiful night. Remember when we were little? Dad would wrap us up in blankets and bring us outside to look at the stars before bed?"

"Ah, yes, those were the days," Paul and Jarred said in unison, their voices tinged with nostalgia.

"You'd put one of us on each arm, and the last one got a piggyback ride," Maddie continued with a laugh. "We used to argue for hours over whose turn it was for the piggyback ride. It's funny now, looking back, how big a deal that seemed to us."

"Where has the time gone?" Tyler said wistfully. "You kids have grown up way too fast."

Dara smiled, her eyes twinkling with a shared memory. "Cari, do you remember when we were kids and started liking boys?"

Cari erupted into laughter. "Oh, how could I forget?"

"What's so funny?" Liza asked, puzzled by their reaction.

Both women, still laughing, replied in unison, "We put

on our own makeup in first grade to impress the boys we liked!"

Dara, catching her breath, added, "What's even funnier is that Joe and Elton dressed up in their 'best' clothes to impress us too. Or so we thought."

Cari couldn't stop giggling. "Joe looked like a walking watermelon! He wore these bright green dress-up pants that were way too big and baggy, paired with one of his dad's black ties over a light pink, freshly ironed t-shirt. It was absolutely ridiculous!"

"Oh, and Elton," Dara interjected, her voice full of amusement.

"Do you remember what he wore, Cari?"

"Yes, I sure do." Cari grinned as the laughter continued to fill the night air.

"He wore a bright. No, let me rephrase. It was a full-on neon-yellow dress shirt with salmon-colored pants. It was like he stepped out of a tropical fruit basket!" Dara exclaimed, her laughter echoing against the farm buildings.

"Oh, and don't forget," Cari added, barely able to keep a straight face, "they both slicked their hair back like they were trying to be the coolest kids in school. They looked more like characters out of an old comedy sketch than 'cool kids.'"

"One of their moms, probably Joe's mom, took a picture of the four of us that day," Dara said, a wistful smile crossing her face. "I wonder what happened to Joe and Elton. Do you think they still remember that day as vividly as we do?"

"I think I heard something about Elton becoming a lawyer

and moving to New Mexico," Cari replied thoughtfully. "But honestly, I have no idea what Joe's up to these days. He just sort of disappeared off the radar."

"Wow," Dara interjected, her voice tinged with nostalgia. "I can't believe that happened so long ago. It still feels like it was just yesterday."

"Well, you guys are old, so maybe it feels closer than it actually is," Jarred quipped, trying to lighten the mood with a cheeky grin.

"You better watch yourself, young man," Mr. Lerian said, pointing a finger at Jarred but smiling warmly. "Before you know it, you'll be sitting around with your own half-grown kids, telling them these same stories and realizing how quickly time flies."

The evening sky filled with laughter as the group settled back into their chairs. It was a night brimming with blessings, warmth, and joy. Family and friends continued swapping stories and reliving cherished memories, their voices weaving together a tapestry of shared experiences that stretched far into the night, a night none of them would soon forget.

Macy

Macy sat on the thin mattress of her cot, staring at the cinder block wall of her juvenile detention cell. The air smelled like bleach and something stale, like old regrets clinging to the corners of the room. The fluorescent light above buzzed softly, a never-ending reminder that night and day didn't mean much in here.

She traced a finger over the rough stitching on her jumpsuit, her jaw clenched tight. She hated this place. Hated the dull gray walls, the scratchy blankets, the way the guards watched her like she was some kind of caged animal. But most of all, she hated the silence. It pressed against her, heavier than the accusations in court, heavier than the disappointment in her mother's brief visit.

Her mother had only come once, and she barely looked at Macy the entire time. Instead, she'd just sighed, shook her head, and muttered, "I don't even know what to do with you anymore." That had been a week ago, and Macy hadn't seen her since.

Not that she was surprised.

She curled her fingers into fists, digging her nails into her palms until they stung. She was used to being alone. She'd been alone her whole life, except for JoAnna. But even JoAnna wasn't here now.

Macy squeezed her eyes shut.

She hadn't meant for things to go this far. She just wanted to shake them up a bit, to make the McDowe family feel the way she felt every single day: small, overlooked, powerless. She hadn't thought about the way fire spread, how once it took hold, it had a life of its own. She just wanted to see the flames, to watch something crumble under her control for once.

But now she was the one crumbling.

Her hands trembled as she exhaled sharply, shaking her head as if that could rid her of the thoughts clawing at her mind.

A voice cut through the silence. "Macy."

She looked up. One of the detention center workers, a woman, Ms. Carter, stood at the bars. She wasn't like the guards. She didn't treat Macy like she was just another criminal. She actually looked her in the eyes when she spoke.

"You've got visitors," Ms. Carter said.

Macy's stomach clenched. She didn't move right away. Her mom wouldn't be back. And JoAnna? Who knows where her relationship stands with her sister after this.

"Who?" Macy finally muttered.

Ms. Carter didn't answer, just motioned for her to follow.

With a sigh, Macy pushed herself off the cot and followed her down the hall, her worn-out sneakers scuffing against the floor. The walk felt longer than usual, her heart pounding harder with every step.

And then she saw them. Maddie and Jarred McDowe.

They were sitting on the other side of the glass, waiting. Macy stopped in her tracks.

She felt something heavy settle in her chest, something she didn't have a name for. Anger? No. Guilt? Maybe.

She forced herself forward, dropping into the chair across from them. The phone on the wall loomed beside her. She didn't want to pick it up. She didn't want to hear whatever they had to say.

But Maddie was looking at her, not with hatred, not with disgust, but with something else. Something that made Macy's stomach twist.

She swallowed hard and reached for the receiver.

"You came all the way here to tell me how awful I am?" she muttered, gripping the phone tighter than necessary.

Maddie shook her head. "No. We came to talk."

Macy scoffed. "About what? How I ruined your life? How you want to see me rot in here?"

Jarred leaned forward. His jaw was tight, but his eyes weren't full of rage like she expected. "No, Macy. We want to talk about forgiveness."

Macy flinched. Forgiveness?

She let out a bitter laugh, shaking her head. "That's rich."

But Maddie didn't flinch. "We mean it." Macy stared at

them.

And for the first time in a long time, she didn't have a single thing to say.

Knocking On Redemption's Door

The conversation sat with Macy long after Maddie and Jarred left.

Forgiveness. It was a word that had never meant much to her.

No one had ever asked for her forgiveness. And no one had ever offered it to her, either.

She lay awake in her cell that night, staring at the ceiling, replaying Maddie's words over and over. *We don't hate you. We don't want revenge. We just want you to know that you don't have to stay this person forever.*

Macy didn't know what to do with that.

For so long, she had told herself that she was nothing more than the sum of her anger. That life had dealt her a bad hand, and the only way to survive was to play it rough.

But what if ... what if there was another way?

The next morning, Ms. Carter stopped by her cell again. "You have another visitor."

Macy sat up, her heart thudding against her ribs. It wasn't Maddie or Jarred this time.

It was a man, dressed simply, with kind eyes and a Bible in his hands.

Macy crossed her arms. "I don't do religion."

The man smiled. "That's okay. I just came to talk."

She should have rolled her eyes. She should have told him to leave. But something small, something almost afraid inside her, kept her in her seat.

And for the first time in her life, Macy listened.

An Embittered Heart Cracked

Macy sat stiffly in the cold metal chair, arms crossed as she studied the man in front of her.

He was calm, unshaken by the weight of her glare. His Bible rested in his lap, but he hadn't opened it yet. Instead, he just sat, waiting, as if he knew she needed to speak first.

She wouldn't. She wasn't about to spill her guts to some preacher.

Still, she eyed him warily. "So, what? You're a prison chaplain?"

"Not exactly." The man smiled, leaning forward slightly. "My name's Pastor Greg. Maddie and Jarred asked me to come see you."

Macy's stomach twisted. She should've guessed.

She let out a short, bitter laugh. "Figures. They think they can fix me now?"

Pastor Greg shook his head. “No. They just care about you. And they believe that you don’t have to be stuck in this cycle forever.”

Macy clenched her jaw.

That cycle. The one that started long before the fire. The one that had been shaping her life since childhood: anger, resentment, lashing out, pushing people away before they could leave first.

She hated how much she recognized it.

She shifted uncomfortably in her seat. “So, what? You came here to preach at me?”

Pastor Greg’s smile didn’t fade. “No. I came here to listen.” That made Macy pause.

No one ever listened to her. Not really. People heard her anger, her sarcasm, her bitterness. But no one had ever really wanted to hear what was underneath it.

She swallowed, looking away. “There’s nothing to listen to.” “I don’t believe that.”

Silence stretched between them.

For the first time since being locked up, Macy felt something crack inside her, just a little.

And it terrified her.

The Road to Forgiveness

As the days passed, Macy found herself meeting with Pastor Greg more than she expected. She didn't always talk much, but he never pressured her. He just listened, and when she asked questions, he answered them without judgment.

At first, she resisted. She fought against the idea that she could change, that she could be more than the mistakes that had landed her in juvie. But the McDowe siblings kept showing up. They sent her letters. They made sure she knew they still saw her as a person, not just a criminal.

One afternoon, she sat across from JoAnna in the visitation room.

JoAnna looked rough. Her normally confident posture had sagged, and dark circles clung under her eyes.

"I'm sorry," she said, her voice barely above a whisper. Macy tensed.

JoAnna swallowed hard, gripping the phone tightly. "I should've stopped it. I should've told you no."

Macy's throat tightened. The old part of her wanted to lash out, to say something cruel, to push JoAnna away like she had done with everyone else in her life.

But another part of her that had been chipping away ever since Maddie and Jarred walked into this place held her back.

"I was wrong," Macy finally muttered. JoAnna's eyes filled with tears. "Me too."

They sat in silence, both of them carrying the weight of what they had done.

And for the first time, Macy let herself feel not just the anger, not just the shame, but the possibility that maybe, just maybe, she didn't have to carry it alone.

Fire's Burn

Weeks turned into months.

Juvenile detention wasn't easy. Macy had to navigate social politics, keep her head down, and fight the old instincts to lash out. But something had changed.

Pastor Greg's visits continued. They talked about everything: the fire, her bitterness, her mother, her father leaving.

One day, she finally asked the question that had been gnawing at her.

"Why do they care?" she muttered, staring at the floor. "Why do Maddie and Jarred still check in on me? After everything I did?"

Pastor Greg leaned back in his chair, thoughtful. "Because forgiveness isn't about excusing what happened. It's about breaking the cycle."

Macy frowned. "Breaking the cycle?"

He nodded. "You've been living in pain and anger for

years, Macy. So has JoAnna. But Maddie and Jarred refuse to let that cycle keep going. They've chosen to forgive, not because you deserve it, but because they know what bitterness does to a person. They are forgiving because God first forgave them."

Macy let the words sink in.

She had spent so much of her life believing that pain was power. That hurting others before they could hurt her made her strong.

But where had that gotten her? Alone.

Trapped.

Wearing a jumpsuit in a cold, gray cell. Maybe there was another way.

Maybe it was time to stop running.

JoAnna

JoAnna sat across from Maddie and Jarred in the visitation room. She had expected awkwardness. Resentment. Maybe even anger.

Instead, Maddie smiled. "You sound ... different."

JoAnna scoffed. "Gee, thanks. Orange jumpsuits really bring out my eyes."

Jarred smirked, shaking his head. "That's not what she meant." JoAnna knew.

She felt different. She had been thinking a lot about life.

They talked for a while about school, about life outside these walls, about Macy, who had been changing.

Finally, Maddie's expression grew serious. "JoAnna, we wanted to tell you something."

JoAnna pursed her lips, but Maddie reached for her hand. "We forgive you."

JoAnna stared at her, heart hammering. "Why?"

Jarred leaned forward. "Because we were forgiven first."

JoAnna frowned. "What's that supposed to mean?"

Maddie exhaled. "It means we're not holding onto the anger anymore. And we don't want you to, either. We've been learning a lot about grace, about how God forgives us even when we don't deserve it." JoAnna swallowed.

She wasn't sure she believed in all that church stuff. But for the first time, she wanted to.

She wanted to believe that she could be more than her mistakes. That she could be more than the anger that had ruled her life.

She hesitated. "So ... what do I do?"

Maddie's smile was gentle. "It starts with a choice."

JoAnna took a shaky breath. For years, she had chosen pleasing people. Anger. Bitterness. Isolation. But maybe there was another way. And for the first time, she was ready to take it.

A New Beginning

Macy didn't fully understand it, but something inside her was shifting.

For years, she had blamed everyone else. Her mother. Her father. The world. But maybe it wasn't about blame.

Maybe it was about surrender.

The next morning, she found Pastor Greg in the facility's chapel.

"I think ..." She hesitated, stuffing her hands in her pockets. "I think I want to know more about this forgiveness thing. About God."

Pastor Greg smiled. "Then let's talk."

They sat down, and he walked her through the Gospel, not the watered-down version she had heard in passing, but the real story. How Jesus had taken the weight of every mistake, every sin, and offered grace in return.

Macy swallowed hard. "And it's that simple, Pastor G.?"

Pastor Greg chuckled and nodded. “It’s not about earning it. It’s about accepting it.”

Macy looked down at her hands.

She had spent so much of her life running. Fighting. Trying to prove something to people who didn’t even care.

But maybe she didn’t have to anymore.

Tears burned at the back of her eyes, but she refused to let them fall.

Instead, she took a deep breath and whispered, “I think I want that.”

Pastor Greg’s smile was warm. “Then all you have to do is ask.” Macy closed her eyes.

Returning Home

A year and a half after Macy's sentencing, she stepped out of the juvenile facility. Cool autumn air smacked into her face first.

She was different now. Not perfect. Not completely healed from before she accepted Christ as Lord of her life. But changed.

She saw JoAnna waiting for her by the car, shifting nervously. Their relationship hadn't gone back to how it was. And maybe that was for the best.

"Hey," JoAnna said. Macy nodded. "Hey."

They stood there in silence before JoAnna cleared her throat. "So, uh ... Maddie and Jarred are waiting for us at the farm."

Macy's heart clenched. She had written them letters. Apologized a hundred times over. But seeing them in person again? That was different.

Still, she climbed into the car.

As they drove down the familiar roads, Macy watched the world pass by. It felt … lighter. She wasn't carrying everything alone anymore.

When they pulled up to the McDowes' farm, Maddie and Jarred were already outside, waiting.

Maddie smiled. "Welcome home."

They had never really had a home before, but maybe this was the start of something new.

Walking Into the Unknown

JoAnna shifted her feet on the gravel driveway, hands stuffed into the pockets of the secondhand jacket she'd been given when she left juvie. The air smelled like fresh hay and damp earth, but she could still remember the acrid scent of smoke from that night she had lost herself completely.

Jarred studied her carefully, his arms crossed, his stance at ease.

It was strange seeing him now, knowing what she had done to his family, knowing he had every right to hate her.

But he didn't.

Maddie was the first to break the silence. "Come inside. Mom's got a fresh pot of licorice tea on. Figured you could use something warm after the ride."

Macy hesitated. This was too easy. Too ... forgiving. She

expected anger, bitterness, a cold shoulder at the very least from Mr. and Mrs. McDowe. But here they were, offering her tea.

The sisters were still getting accustomed to all the kindness they were receiving.

Mrs. McDowe greeted her with a small smile, sliding a steaming mug across the table. “Make yourself comfortable and sit down if you wish.”

Macy took a seat, wrapping her hands around the mug. “Thanks.”

The silence that followed wasn’t uncomfortable, but Macy could feel the weight of it. She wasn’t the same girl who had stood in this house before, but that didn’t erase what she had done.

Mrs. McDowe sat across from Macy, studying her with kind but knowing eyes. “You’ve been through a lot.”

Macy stared out the window.

Mrs. McDowe took a slow sip of her coffee. “So have we.”

Macy looked up. “Yeah, because of me.”

Jarred leaned forward, resting his arms on the table. “Because of what happened, yeah. But not just you.”

Macy frowned.

Maddie spoke next, her voice careful. “You weren’t the only one who was hurting. We were just hurting in different ways.”

Macy shifted in her seat. “That doesn’t excuse what I did.”

“No,” Maddie agreed. “But it explains it. And understanding is the first step toward healing.”

Macy let that sit for a moment, her fingers tightening around the warm mug. "I don't know how to fix it," she admitted.

"You start by letting God do the fixing," Mrs. McDowe said gently.

Field Day

A week later, Macy and JoAnna found themselves standing at the edge of the McDowe fields, watching as Jarred, Paul, and Maddie worked the land.

Jarred approached, wiping sweat from his brow. "You're just gonna stand there, or you wanna help?"

Macy raised a brow. "You're really asking us to help on your farm?"

Jarred shrugged. "Why not? Might do you some good."

Macy scoffed but hesitated. Then, with a sigh, she stepped forward. "Alright. What should I do?"

Jarred handed the girls each a pair of gloves and pointed to the bales of hay that needed stacking. "Start there."

JoAnna grabbed the first bale, the weight surprising her. "This is ridiculous."

Jarred smirked. "Welcome to farm life."

Maddie chuckled from a few feet away. "You'll get used to it." JoAnna rolled her eyes but kept working.

As she lifted another bale, she glanced up at the sky, feeling the warmth of the sun on her face.

Weight of the Past

Macy wiped sweat from her brow, her arms aching from the weight of the hay bales. It wasn't just the physical exhaustion that weighed her down. It was everything else. The guilt. The memories. The knowledge that she was standing on the very land she had tried to destroy.

The McDowe farm had survived, but she and JoAnna had left a scar. And scars didn't just disappear.

"You're slowing down," Jarred teased, tossing another bale onto the stack.

Macy shot him a glare. "Give me a break. I didn't exactly spend my time in juvie getting jacked."

Maddie laughed from where she stood beside the truck. "Could've fooled me. You're doing better than I expected."

"Actually, you girls aren't just free labor until you complete all your community hours. You've become part of our family."

Macy rolled her eyes but felt an odd warmth at their words. They were treating her like she belonged.

She just wasn't sure if she deserved that.

As the sun started to dip below the horizon, Mrs. McDowe called them in for supper. The kitchen was filled with the rich scent of roast chicken and fresh biscuits, and JoAnna hesitated at the door, suddenly unsure.

Jarred nudged her shoulder. "You coming or what?"

JoAnna swallowed hard. "I-yeah."

She stepped inside, feeling the warmth of the McDowes' home wrap around her.

The meal was quiet at first, the sound of forks clinking against plates filling the space. But as the conversation flowed, Macy and JoAnna found themselves drawn in. They laughed at Paul's teasing. They listened as Mr. McDowe talked about the unpredictable weather. They sat at a table they once thought they had no place at.

One Step at a Time

The next Sunday, Macy and JoAnna sat in a wooden pew, shifting uncomfortably as the church filled around them. The McDowes had invited them, and they had said yes.

They glanced at the stained-glass windows, the way the morning light poured through them. People were greeting one another, laughter filling the air. It was so different from anything they had ever known.

Maddie leaned over. "You okay?"

Macy forced a smirk. "Just waiting for Jesus to walk in the doors."

Maddie grinned and gave her a side hug.

The service began with music swelling around the congregation. Macy didn't know the words to the songs, but she couldn't help but smile widely.

Then the pastor spoke. It was Pastor Greg! He talked about redemption. About second chances. About how no one was ever too far gone.

Macy's guilt started dissipating. She could be someone new.

New Life

Macy stepped out of the church, blinking against the bright afternoon sun. The fresh spring air filled her lungs, but she still felt like she couldn't quite catch her breath.

Finally, Macy let out a breath. "So what happens now?"

Jarred shoved his hands in his pockets. "Now you live. You grow. You learn what it means to walk with Him."

Macy nodded slowly. "That sounds ... terrifying."

Maddie laughed. "It's not always easy, but you don't have to do it alone. We're here. And more importantly, God's always here."

Macy chewed on her lip. It still didn't seem real. For so long, she had been carrying this guilt. From her past. From her mistakes. From herself.

A Vision Beyond Sight

Even though life had become busy and their paths diverged, it felt as though nothing had truly changed whenever the McDowes came together. The bond they shared was unshakable, a comforting constant amidst the whirlwind of their growing commitments and dreams.

The McDowe farm was thriving and expanding with new ventures. Jarred had decided to become a therapist specializing in helping burn survivors. Paul, now a high school senior, was deeply committed to following in his father's footsteps, preparing to take over the family farm one day. Maddie, on the other hand, was carving a unique path of her own. Her paintings were garnering international recognition, and her talent had been "discovered" just a year prior. In that short time, she had traveled to every state in the U.S., her art resonating with audiences far and wide. It was feasible for her to travel without her parents because there was a foundation that hired aides for blind people who want their independence but also need or want to travel.

The Seeing Success Foundation (SSF) was founded by a couple who had twin sons born blind and realized that there was very little external support to set their sons up for independence in life. Macy became an integral part of SSF's success since graduating from high school and earning her degree in social work from a local community college. JoAnna landed a job right out of high school working at a homeless shelter just twenty minutes from the outskirts of Marinette.

Despite the excitement of her burgeoning career and the thrill of traveling, Maddie often found herself longing for the serenity of home. The fresh, crisp country air, the comforting hum of the farm, and the warmth of her family called to her. Her mother, her steadfast companion, often drove her to painting events, staying with her when possible or returning to pick her up at the end of a busy week.

As Thanksgiving approached, Maddie's anticipation grew. She dreamed of sitting around the table with her family, sharing stories, laughter, and God's love. Her artwork during this period reflected her gratitude, with paintings dedicated to the things she cherished most: her family, her friends, and the extraordinary journey she had embarked upon. One particularly poignant piece depicted her loved ones gathered around a Thanksgiving table, their faces glowing with joy and togetherness.

The three weeks leading up to Thanksgiving flew by. Maddie was staying in a hotel near the ocean in Cape Town, Massachusetts, and though this was her third time visiting the sea, its vastness of sounds continued to captivate her. She found herself researching ocean life, intrigued by its mysteries and beauty.

One morning, as Maddie stepped out of her hotel room with her white cane, she heard hurried footsteps and a voice to her right.

"Hello, Miss McDowe," the voice called warmly. Maddie turned to hear a middle-aged woman approaching her with a hopeful expression. "My name is Mary Hutchens. My daughter is a huge fan of yours. We've been staying here all week for her doctor's appointments. She doesn't know you're here, but I believe there's a special reason why our paths have crossed this week."

Mary paused, her voice shaking slightly with emotion. "You see, my daughter is blind too. She lost her eyesight gradually due to an incurable condition called macular degeneration. When your story aired on the news last year, it was the first time I saw her face light up in years. Since then, you're all she talks about. Meeting you is her biggest dream, and I think you might be her only hope."

Maddie felt a lump form in her throat. "I was just about to head home for the holidays," she said gently, "but I'd be honored to meet her. Let me call the airline to catch a later flight and let my parents know I'll be delayed. After that, I'd love to meet your daughter."

Tears welled up in Mary's eyes as she nodded gratefully. "Thank you so much. Her name is Aria. I'll make sure she's ready while you make your calls, but I won't ruin the surprise!"

When they reached Mary and Aria's room, Maddie set her bags down near the entryway and took a seat across from where Aria was sitting.

"Hi, Aria," Maddie said softly. "My name's Maddie."

As soon as the words left her lips, Aria leapt from her chair and flung herself into Maddie's arms. The embrace was warm and tight, and tears streamed down Aria's face as if a dam had broken. Her face glowed with pure joy, like a beacon of light piercing through years of darkness.

The two remained in that embrace for a long moment, a silent testament to the profound impact of hope and connection. For Aria, it was the beginning of a memory she would carry forever, a moment where her dream became a beautiful reality.

"Oh, Maddie," Aria said, her voice trembling with emotion. "You are my hero. You've defied the odds and always come out better, braver, and stronger. I've followed your story since it aired on YouTube. I've dreamed of this moment for what feels like forever. And now you're here. I mean, you are really here in front of me! I can't believe it. May I touch your face to see what you look like?"

Maddie smiled awkwardly but welcoming, her heart touched by Aria's words. "Of course, you can," she replied gently. "And if it's okay with you, may I do the same, Aria?"

"Yes, yes, yes!" Aria exclaimed, her excitement unhinged.

They sat close, sharing a moment that felt both profound and natural. Aria's hands moved with delicate precision as she explored Maddie's features, while Maddie traced Aria's face with the same gentle care.

For hours, the two talked and laughed, sharing stories about life, dreams, and the challenges they had faced. As the sun dipped below the horizon, Maddie reluctantly rose to her feet.

"Aria, meeting you has been truly special," Maddie said, her voice filled with warmth. "But I need to head home now. Thank you for reminding me why I do what I do."

Aria flung herself into Maddie's arms, tears of joy streaming down her face. "Thank you, Maddie, for spending time with me."

Maddie left with a full heart, catching a train to Appleton, Wisconsin. James was waiting for her at the station, leaning casually against the car.

"So," he said with a teasing grin as he helped her with her bags, "remind me why you canceled your flight again?"

Maddie chuckled. "Because a little girl needed my friendship more than I needed that flight."

James shook his head with a smile. "You're something else, Mads. A sunflower in a world full of thorns."

Maddie giggled. "Oh, why thank you, fine sir."

Bountiful Blessings

Thanksgiving had finally arrived, and the McDowe kitchen was alive with the enticing aromas of roasted turkey, brown sugar-baked beans, buttery corn, warm garlic bread, and a variety of freshly baked pies waiting for dessert. Fifteen people were cozily gathered in the McDowe home that day, filling the space with laughter, warmth, and gratitude. The family and friends came together to rejoice and give thanks, their hearts full of praise for God's abundant blessings.

Before the meal began, they all bowed their heads in unison as Mr. McDowe led the prayer:

> *Dear God, we are all gathered here today to give thanks to you for your incredible gifts. Simply being alive in your world, Lord, is a blessing. Thank you for this farm and the beauty that surrounds us.*
>
> *Thank you for bringing our families together here*

today. Thank you for blessing us with good health, for guiding us daily, and for this feast we're about to enjoy. Above all, thank you for the endless love you so graciously give.

Amen.

Tyler sat at the head of the table, with Dara to his left and his parents seated beside her. Grandpa Richard sat next to Paul, followed by Greyson and Allison. On one side of Macy was Allison, and on the other side of Macy sat JoAnna. Jarred sat at the opposite end of the table. On Tyler's right sat Mr. Lerian, with Cari next to her husband. James was seated beside Cari, while Maddie sat on his other side. Liza was nestled between Maddie and Jarred, completing the cozy circle.

After the hearty main course, the group transitioned to playing euchre, a popular card game played in Wisconsin. Two games unfolded around the table: Tyler and Dara faced off against James and Liza, while Maddie and Greyson teamed up against Allison and Jarred. Meanwhile, Grandma Noel and Grandpa Richard competed against Paul and Mike, with Cari rounding out the lineup. The winners of each game would later challenge each other, intensifying the excitement. The room buzzed with competitive energy as laughter and the occasional witty remark, often from Maddie, filled the air. James couldn't help but find her sharp sense of humor particularly charming.

After hours of spirited gameplay, it was time for dessert. Dara and Cari had outdone themselves, preparing five pies to satisfy the crowd. Alongside the classic pumpkin pie, there were black cherry, blueberry, peach, and everyone's favorite, lemon meringue. The evening concluded with the women working together to clean up while the men headed outside to chop firewood. With winter fast approaching and *The Farmer's Almanac* predicting a harsh season, they knew they needed ample wood to keep the family warm in the coming months.

Whiteout

The seasons were shifting, and winter had firmly taken hold. The McDowe family was at home, except for Jarred, who was away speaking at a three-day conference. His absence was felt, but everyone knew he wouldn't be back until December 13. In the meantime, life continued at the McDowe household. The Christmas tree stood tall in the living room, its ornaments twinkling in the soft glow of the string lights. Everything seemed peaceful and in order.

Outside, a thick blanket of snow covered the ground, measuring a full foot in depth. The temperature had remained steady at twenty-four degrees Fahrenheit for the past month, keeping the cold manageable and predictable. The firewood had been cut and neatly stacked earlier in the season, providing reassurance that the family was prepared for the winter ahead.

Maddie and Paul balanced their schoolwork during the day with their responsibilities on the farm at night. Maddie had grown into an exceptional cook, so she often took charge of dinner preparations, crafting hearty meals that brought warmth to their evenings. Paul and Dara handled feeding the calves, ensuring the young animals were cared for. Tyler took on everything else, managing the larger tasks that kept the farm running smoothly.

It was December 3, and the family was counting down the days until Jarred's return in ten days. Despite this, Tyler remained vigilant, frequently scanning the horizon for any signs of trouble. He had learned from experience that the weather could turn without warning, and his instincts told him to stay prepared.

Two days before Jarred's expected arrival, on December 11, the quiet was abruptly shattered. The morning began like any other, with Tyler and Dara outside tending to chores around five o'clock. The air was cold but calm, until it wasn't.

Without warning, the wind began to howl, gaining strength rapidly. Snow started falling in thick, relentless sheets, spilling from the sky in torrents. Tyler paused, listening intently as a low rumbling noise echoed from the north side of the barn.

"What was that?" he muttered to himself, his voice barely audible over the rising wind.

He hurried toward the barn, his boots crunching in the snow. When he reached Dara, he saw the damage. A section of the barn wall had been torn away, leaving part of the structure exposed. Dara was kneeling on the ground, staring up at the destruction in stunned silence.

"Dara!" Tyler shouted, grabbing her arm. "We need to move!"

The wind was now so fierce that they had to yell to hear each other. The snowflakes came down so fast and thick that visibility was reduced to mere feet.

"The calves are fed," Tyler said, his voice straining over the roar of the storm. "I'm heading to the tool shed to grab lumber and tools. Go wake Paul. We need his help out here!"

"I can't leave you!" Dara protested, her voice tinged with fear. "We won't make it back to the house in this weather!"

"You have to try, Dara. We can't do this alone," Tyler insisted, his tone firm. "Now, go!"

Reluctantly, Dara turned and began her trek back to the house. The wind battered her small frame, knocking her to the ground multiple times. Each step felt like a monumental effort as she pushed through the snow. Finally, she was within ten feet of the house when Paul came running out the door, his face filled with concern.

"Mom! You need to get inside," Paul said urgently. "I'll go help Dad. Where is he?"

"How did you know something was wrong?" Dara asked, catching her breath.

"I heard the wind," Paul replied. "Come on, I'll help you to the house."

"Okay," Dara said, nodding. "Your father was in the green tool shed. He needs help fixing the north side wall of the barn. Before you come back inside, check that everything else is secure so we don't have to go out again unless absolutely necessary. I think this storm's going to stick around for a while."

"Got it," Paul said. "Make sure we have enough firewood, okay? If we don't, call Dad or me, and we'll get more."

"I will," Dara assured him. "Be careful, honey." She kissed the top of his head gently.

"Always," Paul replied with a quick smile. "Love ya, Mom."

Paul made his way to the barn, where he found Tyler bent over, catching his breath.

"Dad! Are you okay?" Paul called out.

"I'm fine," Tyler replied, straightening up. "Just got the wind knocked out of me."

Paul managed to secure a tarp with minor tears in the busted-up barn corner to help keep the storm out. It took all of Paul's strength to stay on top of the ladder while snow and wind battered him. He lost his balance a couple of times but managed to catch himself each time.

Before Tyler got into the tractor to collect extra firewood for the fireplace, he took a roll of twine and tied it from the barn to the house, ensuring they could still reach the animals if needed. Once Tyler had secured the firewood, he fed the cows extra TMR mixture.

By the time they finished, both father and son were dripping with sweat and gasping for air, but relieved. The repairs were solid for the time being, the animals were safe, and the house was going to stay cozy. As they headed back to the house, the storm continued to rage, but the McDowes knew they had done everything possible to prepare for whatever winter had in store.

Paul checked his phone, and sure enough, his mom had texted them, saying they needed more firewood. They both jumped onto a four-wheeler, which was hooked up to trailers, and drove it down to the stack of wood they had cut back on Thanksgiving. They filled their trailers to the brim and brought them back to the house. Maddie and Dara met them at the door and helped unload the trailers. Maddie, with ease, grabbed the pieces of wood and carried them into the garage attached to the house. By the time the trailers were empty, visibility had become nearly impossible, so they tucked the four-wheelers away in the garage. Finally, they found themselves back inside their cozy house, the smell of sizzling bacon wafting through the air.

"Sure is crazy out there," Tyler said as he rubbed his hands together to warm them.

"Yeah, we fixed the barn and gave the cattle extra feed, so we won't have to go back out until tomorrow," Paul replied. "But we will need all hands on deck to milk the cows and feed the calves again tonight."

"I'm just glad you're back in here, out of that cold weather," Dara said, wrapping Tyler in a loving hug. It was Saturday, a day usually reserved for cleaning the house and playing a family game. They were grateful for the extra time together, but as the hours passed, everyone grew increasingly anxious, especially as the storm showed no signs of letting up. Dara sat in a chair, knitting a shawl, while Maddie painted, and Tyler and Paul discussed plans for a new sheep barn they wanted to build come spring.

The wind howled wickedly outside. Tyler turned on the news and heard reports of a major blizzard heading their way.

"Those blasted weathermen," Tyler muttered in frustration. "I tell you, they seem to only be good for one thing: reading screens."

The temperatures dropped more than thirty degrees in less than twenty-four hours. Paul, Dara, and Tyler bundled up and went outside to tend to the chores.

The calves' hutches were already packed with warm straw, and they all had coats over them for protection. The only group of cattle they truly worried about in this weather was the pregnant cows and heifers. They put barricades in front of the big barn doors in case the wind blew them in, and they covered the wider slats in the wood with old blankets. When they finished, they worked together to create a makeshift area for the newborn calves.

By the time they returned to the house, their hands were tinged a bluish-white from the cold. Their cheeks were red, and icicles hung from the brims of their winter hats. These hats had flaps to cover their ears and a visor, much like a baseball cap, allowing them to see in the blinding snow.

After Dara drew three footbaths, she called Jarred. He didn't know when he'd be home, but he prayed it would be soon. He told his mom that the firefighters in the town were working tirelessly to dig out everyone's homes and businesses from the blizzard. Since the hotel was located on the outskirts of the city, it would be last on the list. Blizzards were hitting all across the country, including parts of the South that rarely saw snow, let alone experienced a full-blown blizzard. It was December 10. The family tried to take their minds off the storm by reading, playing games, and telling stories, all while sitting around the warmth of the wood stove.

In the living room, everyone sat huddled together, wrapped in blankets to shield themselves from the cold. With every new piece of wood gently set into the fire, the crackling grew louder, and the warmth from the flames sent embers dancing in the air. The days seemed to stretch on, growing slower and slower with each passing hour. They filled the silence of the house with songs, singing joyously to break the unbearable stillness that seemed to consume them. By this point, the snow had accumulated so much that every time Tyler returned from plowing, it looked more and more like their farm was perched on top of a deep valley, surrounded by walls of white.

The blizzard raged on for nine long days. When the storm finally subsided, everyone realized there was much cleaning up to do before settling into the winter season. It was now just a week before Christmas, and Jarred still hadn't made it home. During the height of the blizzard, most airports around the nation had been shut down to protect the safety of travelers. Slowly, though, the airports began to reopen, one by one.

The phone finally rang. "Mom?"

"Jarred, baby! I'm so glad to hear your voice. What's going on? Is everything okay?"

"Yes, Mom. Everything's great. I'm just now boarding a plane to come home. I'll be landing at seven tomorrow morning."

"Ahh! That is so wonderful, Jarred! I'm so looking forward to having you back home, sweetheart. Make sure you make wise choices and stay safe. I love you."

"Bye, Mom. I love you, too."

As Dara hung up the phone, a joyful squeal escaped her lips. "Jarred will be home tomorrow morning! You know what? I'm going to bake his favorite tonight, chocolate cherry cake, in celebration of the whole McDowe family being reunited once again!"

"Good idea, honeycakes," Tyler said with a grin, giving Dara a quick peck on the lips.

A Refreshed Heart

Their hearts were full of love and contentment as they all sat around the table, chatting and eating cake.

"I'm so glad all three of my babies are home again," Dara said with a nostalgic sigh. "I can't believe you're all so grown up. It feels like just yesterday that I was carrying Maddie around in a sling while Paul and Jarred were playing leapfrog around the house."

Jarred chuckled and added, "I remember that. I was about five years old when Maddie was in the sling, and you got cornered by a mother sow in the hog barn. You cried out because she was charging at you, and there was nowhere for you to go. As soon as I heard you scream, I ran as fast as I could out of the barn, yelling for Dad. He heard me and jumped into the pen to save you. That was pretty epic." He gave his dad a crisp high-five, still grinning.

"You know, Jarred," Tyler said with a smile, "by the grace of God, Maddie just ended up with a few scratches.

That could have been a lot worse."

"Tell us about your adventures at the conference, Jarred," his dad asked, eager to hear more.

"Well, let me take you back to the very beginning," Jarred began. "I had just arrived at the hotel after flying in from the Reno-Tahoe International Airport. After checking in at the front desk, I headed to my room, which was incredible. It had crystal-clear glass window panes, a full kitchen, and live-action framed pictures of nature scenes. It was hands down the best hotel room I've ever stayed in. The conference was called 'Keep Moving Forward,' and it was all about how to center conversations on Christ in therapy sessions. It was extremely encouraging and helpful.

"We, as McDowes, never have to think twice about asking God for help, but it seems there are so many people out there who need encouragement to seek God's guidance. Telling my story and spreading God's Word is something that truly resonates with others. It's kind of strange, actually.

"Negativity kills every smile in a room. That's my biggest lesson learned since meeting so many people and listening to their stories. Anyway, enough with the squirrel tangent. On the third day of the conference, the blizzard began, and the city was actually shut down for a period of time because there were so many accidents. Not all of them were vehicle collisions. Many were caused by the powerful wind, which blew people and cars right off the road!

"I hadn't turned on the news during the conference, so this was a shock to me. There was so much snow, and all the exit doors in the building were blocked. Many people who had come just for the day to attend the conference weren't staying in the hotel, so the place quickly became overcrowded and chaotic. Over one hundred temporary beds made from blankets and sheets were set up in the entryway and hallways. During mealtimes, the dining hall was packed. Talk about being uncomfortable. I do not like being surrounded.

"One thing that really struck me was the incredible kindness of a stranger. There was a family that ran out of money to pay for their meal, and someone else immediately stepped up to cover their bill. It was such a simple act, but it really showed how the community rallied together to make things work. My first thought when we were trapped was that there would be a mad rush for supplies and that people might get hurt, but that wasn't the case. Instead, the community created in the hotel made up games to keep everyone, but especially the children, entertained, and it worked out surprisingly well.

"The days seemed to stretch on, but I think God really taught me to appreciate the little, mundane moments of everyday life. Eventually, the fire department came to shovel us out, and here I am. It was an experience I'll never forget."

"That does sound like an adventure, Jarred! It really is good to have you back home, though," Mrs. McDowe said and wrapped her adult son in a mama bear hug.

As Christmas approached, the McDowe house was filled with songs of joy and wonder:

Joy to the world, the Lord is come.
Let earth receive her King;
Let every heart prepare Him room,
And heaven and nature sing.
And heaven and nature sing.
And heaven, and heaven, and nature sing.
Oh-oh-oh, Joy to the world!

Time of Change

Since Thanksgiving, Maddie's dreams had changed. One, in particular, left her confused. It was a recurring dream, happening one night, then the next, and again the night after that.

In the dream, James Lerian appeared, and it always followed the same pattern. It was just the two of them, walking toward each other from opposite ends of the Lerians' sunflower field. Eventually, they would meet in the middle of the field. Without exchanging a single word, they lay down side by side and gazed up at the sun, shaded by the sunflowers. James took Maddie's hand, his touch soft yet firm, smooth, and warm. She found herself liking the sensation. And then, the dream would end.

Each time Maddie woke up from that dream, she was drenched in sweat. Despite her clammy skin, a chill ran through her body, leaving her feeling cold and alone.

Early one morning, she was overcome with a pounding headache and a strange sense of unease. She yelled for her mother. Moments later, Dara bolted into the room.

"What's wrong, dear one?" Dara asked, her voice tinged with alarm.

"I'm freezing, but I'm sweating too. My head feels like it's going to explode. The pain just won't stop," Maddie groaned.

Dara's concern deepened as she looked at her daughter. "Stay right here. I'll grab the thermometer," she said, rushing to the bathroom.

When Dara returned and checked Maddie's temperature, the reading made her gasp. It read 105.9! Her heart pounding, Dara screamed for Tyler, but he was already out tending to the morning chores. Jarred and Paul weren't home either.

Desperate, Dara started calling everyone she could think of. She tried Cari, but it went straight to voicemail. She called Liza, then Allison, and finally Greyson, but no one answered. It was three in the morning, and they were all likely still asleep. Frustrated and running out of options, Dara's last hope was James. With tears streaming down her pale, sunken cheeks, she dialed his number. Miraculously, he answered.

"Mrs. McDowe?" James mumbled, his voice heavy with sleep.

"Ja-ames," Dara stuttered, barely able to say his name. "Maddie's sick. She has a terrible fever. Please come quickly. We need to get her to the hospital."

"I'm on my way," James replied hurriedly, rubbing his

eyes and throwing on a deep blue sweatshirt and green khakis that were draped over the side of his bed as he sprang into action.

James arrived in record time, leaving his vehicle running and bursting into their house, then Maddie's bedroom, to carry her to the car. He helped Dara prop Maddie up with pillows to ensure her ride to the hospital was as comfortable as possible. Dara sat in the back with Maddie, making urgent phone calls, one to alert the hospital to their arrival and another to inform Tyler of the situation.

When James pulled up to the hospital entrance, two nurses were already waiting. Gently, James lifted Maddie's frail body out of the car and placed her on the stretcher the nurses had brought out. They quickly wheeled her inside while Dara stayed behind to speak with the receptionist. James parked the car and jogged inside, just in time to hear Dr. Lapel deliver devastating news.

"If we don't operate immediately, Maddie has a very high chance of dying within the hour," the doctor explained. He went on to reveal that the emergency surgery Maddie had undergone after the fire had led to an undetected infection. This infection had caused a brain aneurysm, and now, her life depended on immediate action.

When Dara joined them in the room, Dr. Lapel briefly explained the situation before whisking Maddie away to surgery.

The operation lasted an hour and a half. During that time, James helped unpack some of the emergency bags Dara had brought from the house. Once everything was settled, he drove home to get a few hours of sleep before returning with his family to visit Maddie.

As James drove home, memories flooded his mind. He passed familiar places where he and Maddie had spent time together over the years, including the Lincoln Restaurant, Amber's Pancake Parlor, and Gary's Greasy Garage. Each spot held a special memory.

Gary, the garage owner, had once let Maddie pick out scraps of metal and rusty tools to create a picture frame for James' tenth birthday. The frame, holding a photo of them dirt biking, still hung proudly in his room.

As James continued down the road, a realization hit him with the force of a speeding train. He loved Maddie, not as a sister or a friend, but in a deeper, more romantic way. Tears welled up in his eyes, and for the first time in a long time, he let them fall. The sensation was unfamiliar, but it felt right.

He took a deep, steadying breath and whispered, "God, I love her. Please don't take her to be with You now."

When James got home, the comforting aroma of breakfast greeted him as his mom stood at the stove, cooking. He briefly explained what had happened, his voice heavy with emotion, before heading back to bed for a couple of hours of much-needed rest.

Meanwhile, Dara updated Tyler on Maddie's condition. As soon as he finished his chores, Tyler rushed to the hospital. He arrived just as Maddie was wheeled out of surgery and into the recovery room. Bringing along a few more items from the house that Dara had requested, Tyler settled in to wait with the others.

It took several hours before Maddie began to wake from

the effects of anesthesia. By then, the Lerian family had arrived, just in time to see her slowly regain consciousness.

Maddie found herself surrounded by her loved ones in the hospital room. As her eyes fluttered open, she was met with a faint glimmer of light. Slowly, the blurry outlines of her family and friends came into focus. She felt disoriented and confused, her voice trembling as she called out.

"Mom?!" Maddie cried.

Dara immediately touched her daughter's hand. "I'm right here, baby. I'm right here. We're all here. You're okay now. You just woke up from surgery."

"Mom ... is that you?" Maddie asked, her voice laced with uncertainty.

"Yes, sweetheart, it's me," Dara reassured her gently.

Within seconds, Maddie's vision sharpened, and she could clearly see the faces around her. Maddie choked up as she looked at each person in turn, softly speaking their names.

"Mom ... Dad ... Liza ... Allison ... Cari ... Greyson ... James. I ca-can SEE you!"

Her gaze stopped when it landed on James. He looked different from how she remembered him. The roundness of his chubby cheeks had been replaced by defined, handsome cheekbones. His hair was darker, with a natural wave that framed his face magnificently. He wore a blue-and-white checkered button-up shirt that subtly showcased the muscles he hadn't had the last time she laid eyes on him.

As Maddie took in the sight of her loved ones, tears welled up in her eyes, mirroring the joyous tears streaming down their faces.

"Well, I haven't seen anyone get their eyesight back after losing it in my fifteen years of practice. There is no sound medical explanation as to why Maddie got hers back. My only explanation is that the infection was affecting her optic nerves, which put enough pressure on her nerves to lose her sight, and when the infection cleared up, the pressure was released, and her eyesight was restored," Dr. Lapel stated. "It was simply a modern phenomenon."

"No, Doctor. It was a miracle from God," Tyler beamed proudly.

A few hours later, Jarred and Paul arrived to visit Maddie.

News of her hospitalization spread quickly through the town. Upon hearing it, Macy and JoAnna felt compelled to act. While Maddie recovered, the Pewasta sisters organized the largest community fundraiser in the town's history. Their efforts paid off. Every one of Maddie's medical bills was covered before she was even discharged. Quietly, the sisters resolved not to let the McDowe family know it was their hard work that erased the financial burden. God had touched their hearts deeply since the incident and trial, and their actions were a testament to that transformation.

Finally, the day came for Maddie to go home.

"James, may I ride home with you?" Maddie asked shyly, the blush in her cheeks unmistakable.

James' heart pounded in his chest as he replied, "Yeah, of course."

"Thank you, James." Maddie carefully swung her legs off the stiff hospital bed, using her hands to steady herself as they touched the cool linoleum floor.

While packing the last of Maddie's clothes into an earl-gray suitcase, Dara turned to her daughter with a warm smile. "Your father and I will take your things home with us. You two can stop for ice cream or something on the way back. That'll give me time to put fresh sheets on your bed so you can settle in and rest comfortably when you get home."

"You don't have to do that, Mom, but thank you," Maddie said.

"Goodbye, darling. We will see you later," Dara walked to Maddie's bedside and kissed her on the forehead.

As Maddie watched her parents leave hand in hand, her eyes wandered over to James, who was kicked back in the recliner with his eyes half shut, and then she noticed something out of character for a dull hospital room. A painting hung on the wall above the recliner. Her breath caught in her throat as she took in the colors, the strokes, the life that seemed to pulse from the canvas. She had felt the paint beneath her fingers, had trusted her hands to move without sight, but seeing it now, with her own eyes, it felt like a miracle from God Himself. Every brushstroke held a memory of uncertainty, of reaching into the unknown and trusting that something beautiful would emerge. The depth of the hues, the way they blended and melted together, shocked her. It wasn't just paint on a canvas; it was proof of something greater than herself. Her fingers twitched, longing to trace the lines she once only knew by touch. The image before her was both familiar and foreign, a reflection of a moment in time when she had surrendered to God's guidance without knowing what the outcome would be. *How could I have done that, God?* she wondered again, her heart swelling with awe. A lump formed in her throat as she blinked away tears, overwhelmed by the realization that even in her darkness, sunshine had found a way through. She was reminded of the verse in Romans: "For from him and through him and for him are all things. To him be the glory forever! Amen." *What a reminder, oh Lord. You sure work in mysterious ways sometimes.*

She turned her focus to James, meeting his gaze with gratitude. Taking a deep breath, she reached for him, and he quickly stepped to her side, his smile reassuring. Together, they walked out of the hospital, waving to the nurses as they passed.

James opened the car door for Maddie. "Are you ready, sunshine?" he asked and shut the car door gently after she got in.

Acknowledgments

My heartfelt thanks to Sierra Jauch for her unwavering support and insight. You didn't write these words, but you helped me think through them, make sense of them, and see how they could truly reach the hearts of readers. Your steady encouragement and perspective have been essential behind this work, helping it become both hard-hitting and sweet to the soul.

About the Author

Laura, author of *Heart of a Dairy Farmer* and *Letters to a Kindred Spirit*, is thrilled to release her second novel. Her writing reflects her passion for sharing stories of family, resilience, and hope, aiming to uplift readers in every season of life.

Laura is dedicated to encouraging others to embrace life's unknowns with courage.

Printed in the United States
by Baker & Taylor Publisher Services